PENGUIN BOOKS

THE SAGA OF DHARMAPURI

O.V. Vijayan was born in 1930 in Palghat, Kerala. The son of a
police officer, he grew up in a camp of armed constabulary which
his father commanded. He had no formal schooling till the age of
twelve and spent this period at home reading fairy-tales. In 1954
he took a Master's degree in English Literature from Madras University and then taught for a while, before becoming a political
cartoonist. His cartoons have appeared in the *Hindu,* the *States-
man, Mathrubhoomi* and the *Far Eastern Economic Review.*
He has also published, in Malayalam, three novels, three novellas,
five collections of stories and several books of political essays.
O.V. Vijayan lives in New Delhi.

O.V. VIJAYAN

The Saga of Dharmapuri

Translated from the Malayalam by the author

PENGUIN BOOKS

Penguin Books (India) Ltd, 72-B Himalaya House 23 Kasturba Gandhi Marg, New Delhi-110 001, India
Penguin Books Ltd, Harmondsworth, Middlesex, England
Viking Penguin Inc, 40 West 23rd Street, New York New York 10010, U.S.A.
Penguin Books Australia Ltd, Ringwood, Victoria, Australia
Penguin Books Canada Ltd, 2801 John Street, Markham Ontario, Canada L3R 1B4
Penguin Books (N.Z.) Ltd, 182-190 Wairau Road, Auckland 10 New Zealand.

First published in Malayalam as *Dharmapuraanam* by D.C. Books, Kottayam 1985
Published in Penguin Books 1988
Copyright © O.V. Vijayan 1985, 1987.
All Rights Reserved.

Made and Printed in India by Ananda Offset Private Limited, Calcutta.
Typeset in Garamond.

To

*Shri Karunakara Guru, the spiritual teacher
of the Shantigiri Ashram, Pothencode, Trivan-
drum, Kerala, who persuaded me to explore
the concept of the teacher and incarnation*

Contents

	Author's Note	. . .	8
	The doggerel of innocence	. . .	9
I	The Stars	. . .	10
II	The President	. . .	11
III	The General	. . .	18
IV	The Kitchen Maid	. . .	29
V	The Merciful Stranger	. . .	36
VI	The Mendicant	. . .	41
VII	The Twice-born	. . .	44
VIII	Laughter Frees the Persuaders	. . .	46
IX	The Tartar Republic and the Eucharist	. . .	51
X	A Cameo of Anti-imperialism	. . .	55
XI	The Getaway	. . .	61
XII	The Man who Sorrowed	. . .	66
XIII	The Legion of the Baptised	. . .	73
XIV	The Slumbering Seeds	. . .	77
XV	The Celestial Birds	. . .	82
XVI	The Night of the Bondsman	. . .	89
XVII	The Stars Set	. . .	94
XVIII	The Old Ones	. . .	99
XIX	The Echoing Valley	. . .	105
XX	The White Overlord	. . .	111
XXI	The Eyes of the Jaahnavi	. . .	117
XXII	The Whore and the General	. . .	122
XXIII	Tinsel on the Coffin	. . .	127
XXIV	The Forests	. . .	133

XXV	The Crystal Prisons	. . . 142
XXVI	The Wayside Scrub	. . . 146
XXVII	The Revelation	. . . 152
XXVIII	The Last Warrior	. . . 156
	Glossary	. . . 160

Author's Note

The original Malayalam title of this book is *Dharmapuraanam,* which is not the same as its English title; *Puraanam* is scriptural folklore, and *Dharma,* much more than secular ethics, a deeper acceptance of what is right in the created order. This is just an example to illustrate the difficulty of translating a novel when the resonances are different, and the languages are far removed from each other as cultural experiences. Yet the barriers are not insurmountable, only it takes much more effort and expertise than when one is dealing with languages that are more closely related.

Dharmapuraanam was begun in 1972, and the weekly journal, *Malayalanadu,* planned to serialize it from July 1975. In June 1975, Prime Minister Indira Gandhi clamped down a State of Emergency, and the serialization had to wait till 1977, when the Emergency was lifted. When the novel began appearing Left and progressive critics cried it down for what they thought was an imperialist slant, and my own constituency of readers was unhappy about its "obscenity". *Dharmapuraanam,* as a book, had to wait till 1985 to find a major Malayalam publisher.

New Delhi   *O.V.Vijayan*
November 1987

8

The doggerel of innocence

Ka twam baale ? Kaanchanamaala.
Kasyaa putri ? Kanakalataaya.
Kin te haste ? Taaleepatram.
Kaavaa rekha ? Ka Kha Ga Gha.

"Who are you, little girl?"
"I am Kaanchanamaala."
"Whose daughter are you?"
"Kanakalata's."
"What do you carry in your hand?"
"Palm leaves."
"What have you written on them?"
"Ka Kha Ga Gha.*"

* (*Ka, Kha, Ga* and *Gha* are the first consonants of the Sanskrit alphabet.)

CHAPTER I

The Stars

Strange stars had risen in darknesses faraway; they raced towards the skies of Dharmapuri, their prophecy written large and luminous in celestial script; their light would touch the earth one baptismal night, and move on, only to return in the far ages to come. Of this plant and animal had knowledge, and they waited in joy.

But in his palace in Shantigrama, capital of Dharmapuri, the President sensed the distant stellar presences, and was gripped by a colic ....

CHAPTER II

The President

As the President squirmed on his throne, and signalled his intent to defecate; a tremorous disquiet passed over the gathering in the Audience Hall, for it was not yet sundown, the Hour of the Second Defecation. Ever since Dharmapuri attained freedom, its President had kept the Hour, defecating at daybreak and sundown, in the rhythm of sovereign nationhood; and these hours were solemnized by the broadcasting network, which played the national anthem to reassure the people that all was well. Children would choke and say, *Ah, the Great Sire defecates,* and mothers, their eyes moist, would invoke for their little ones the grace of the Sovereign Excrement. Only a fortunate few gained actual access to it, and it was these who held power in government, in trade, and in the seats of learning. Even these privileged ones had to obtain the Excrement through elaborate strategies; and then they secured mere smatterings, which they mixed with rare and valuable spices and feasted on with garish ceremony. The press was invited to witness these ritual meals and the nation's newspapers ran pictures of the Excrement-venerators, their smiles broad with the joy of initiation and the stupefaction of dung. In good time the President saw these pictures and was pleased.

Upon the signal from the throne, the President's Military Secretary rose and blew his conch. Its deep bass summoned servants in ornate livery, who wheeled in three cans, mounted on pedestals, to the centre of the Hall. These, the Receptacles of the Sacrament of Dharmapuri — imposing creations in gold and alabaster — were chamber pots of the former Feringhee Empire's *Gobernadors.* As the guests stood by, the President

11

uncovered his behind and ascended the can in the middle, while in the manner of outriders, two young subalterns did likewise on the cans set on either side, to provide the Presidential Excrement with the symbols of retinue. The defecation began to music and ended with a flourish of trumpets and a guardsmen's quadrille. After this six bare-breasted young women washed the posteriors and freshened them with frankincense and myrrh.

The President was early by almost an hour that evening, and as the whispered disquiet grew, the doyen of the press corps made bold to address the President's Press Councillor. 'Sir, this is an unusual hour...'

'The Government has no comment,' the Press Councillor said. 'The Receptacle is open to the gentlemen of the press.'

The newsmen closed in. The white men, as always, had the best positions near the can. The most privileged one was the correspondent of *Prava,* the official newspaper of the Communards of the Red Tartar Republic. After the white men had withdrawn, the rag-tag native press scrambled forward and secured smatterings from the can, which they savoured with evident relish. 'Magnificent,'said one; 'great stability,' said a second. A native pressman who had managed to lay hands on a turdlet no bigger than a peanut, held it between thumb and forefinger and marvelled at its hardness and form. Hard indeed were the turds, and round, for age had greatly constipated the President, and his senile guts passed pellets like those of the mountain goat. (It had even been put down in one of the earlier editions of the Red Tartar Encyclopedia that the President made goat noises while mounting his chosen concubines, a mention which,.for some scholarly reason, subsequent editions did not carry.) The native, after long adoration of the turdlet, spoke, 'Truly, this is as hard as mountain rock. This is our wall against imperialism. Is that not so, White-man-boss?'

The question was put to the *Wild West Times'*correspondent, the most prominent newsman from the White Confederacy. The white man nodded in hasty agreement, holding, even as he did

12

so, a piece of scented gauze to his nose.

'I am glad,' the native said, 'that you do not turn away from reality like many of your countrymen do.'

The native looked menacingly at the gauze, causing the white man to turn crimson. 'Of course, there is no questioning the Sacrament's fragrance. But I have this, er, vicious cold ...'

'I suppose you do. But I presume you have savoured the Sacrament?'

'I would have most certainly wanted to; but this cold has dulled my tongue, and it might be irreverence to ...'

The white man's reply seemed to please the native. The Press Councillor too came up to the white man, smiling, and said, 'But White-man-boss, we take it that you will send your dispatch all the same?'

'Definitely.'

It was no secret that the white men never touched the Excrement, and yet a pretence was kept up by both sides; occasionally the white men did condescend to write about the stability of the Presidency expressed in the stable rhythms of the defecation. A column-inch of desultory reportage appearing in the White Confederate media occasioned great rejoicing in Shantigrama, and, for some inexplicable reason, was prized more than a whole *Prava* supplement.

*

Among the newsmen gathered in the Hall that evening was a young Ruritanian fresh out of university. Untutored in the ways of Dharmapuri, he did an incredible thing. He caught hold of the Press Councillor, and pointing to the can, said, 'A worm! There is a worm in there!'

A secret agent who overheard him, whispered to his colleague, 'The white man is suggesting that our President has a Swiss account!'

The little worm lay embossed on a turd, like a shred of silver embroidery. A native newsman bent over the can and whispered

13

to it, 'Be not afraid, gentle reptile! You are among kin; all of us here live off this substance.'

Shyly the parasite lifted its head for a moment, then sank back again. The Ruritanian repeated, 'There, on that turd!'

'A worm' the Press Councillor said. 'That is blasphemy!'
No native could have blasphemed thus and got away, but this was a white man and he had to be answered. There was much conferring among the officials, and presently the Minister for the Media faced the Ruritanian.

'A worm?' the Minister said. 'That is a canard of Imperialism. The creature in there is a serpent.'

'True,' the *Prava* man said, coming quickly to the Minister's rescue. 'Nowhere have I seen a serpent as wondrous. In the name of the toiling masses of the Tartar Republic, I salute this peaceful and progressive serpent!'

A cheer rose from the assembled guests, and the native Communard scribe went into an ecstasy, crying, 'The serpent is not alone, the Tartar Republic is with us!'

But the Ruritanian kept up his tedious refrain, 'The President has worms!' The native newsmen ringed him round, chanting slogans against imperialism, while at the far end of the great Hall, on an old *Gobernador's* throne, sat the President sucking a bar of candy, relaxing in the great contentment of unburdened bowels.

*

The Palace had indeed been disturbed over the unusual hour of the defecation. And despite all denials, it was true that a premonition of catastrophe had come over the President ...

Meanwhile, far away from the Palace and the city, an unusual traveller was crossing the mountains into Dharmapuri. The soldiers along the frontier saw his gentle smile and waved him in; he wound down the foothills and walked across the plain and through villages where the peasants' and artisans' women fed him. At their doors he stood, ancient yet young, and took their food like a god an offering. Eating the food out of the palms of his hands, he moved on. Soon he was on the road to the city.

This was the city they called Shantigrama, the Village of Peace; an apter re-christening there could not have been for the old capital of the Feringhee Empire's freed colony, for it summed up the spirit abroad in the new nation, its need to improvise selfhood and historical antecedents. As a result the legends of Dharmapuri's ancient forest-dwelling sages and their paths of peace were resurrected. No other country had anything similar to resurrect, and Dharmapuri found itself in a pure and legendary state, with no contender for the spiritual leadership of the world. With peace and wisdom become the protocols of state, it was decided that Dharmapuri would use its armies not to fight but to assuage the ills of the people; armies changed overnight into Congregations of Persuaders, and the murderous encounters with neighbouring countries, which took place ever so often, were designated the Sorrows of Dharmapuri. Rabble-rousers and storm troopers, who, during the days of Empire, had done the State small-time violence, now called themselves Partisans and banded into the Convention of the Holy Spirit and took over the governance of the new republic. Soon after his investiture, the President went on a pilgrimage to the forests where the sages had lived in times gone by; since the sages had worn tree-bark the President too attired himself so on occasions of state. He wore bark for more intimate appearances as well, because certain kinds of bark were known for their aphrodisiac properties. Such were the secular uses of the wisdom of the sages. Soon all the Partisans took to wearing bark, as did the city's tradesmen and pimps; bark had become a fetish of patriotism.

The imperial power replaced with so much that belonged to the spirit, the Convention began looking for an apposite ideology, a spiritual predication of the state; this they eventually found in the legend of the Celestial Birds. This was the story of Shakuntala, around which the play *Shaakuntala* was written;

Shakuntala, the abandoned daughter of an unwed celestial mother, was clothed and fed by the *Shakuntaas,* birds of the forest. The bird as provider caught the fancy of Dharmapuri, whose destitutes were legion; planners and statisticians began talking of the Celestial Birds, and alluding to them in memoranda to the world's credit agencies. Bonds of sympathy grew naturally between international finance and the world of voodoo, and Dharmapuri was never starved of credit.

When the winters came, within warm classrooms the children of the wealthy were taught the lore of the Celestial Birds, while the waifs froze on the sidewalks; television crews from the White Confederacy often sought to portray this, causing great anger among the people, who turned such occasions into street tableaux against imperialism.

*

In a tavern in Shantigrama, a group of citizens became aware of a traveller who sat by himself in a corner. He was coloured like they were, but his features and apparel marked him out as an alien. Then, even as they watched, the wayfarer's dust disappeared from his feet, his locks grew lucent, and a lambent light enveloped him. Frightened by the light, and his gentleness, the citizens huddled together; finding strength in numbers, they rose and advanced on the stranger.

'Who are you, stranger?' asked the leader of the citizens.

He smiled as he replied, 'Call me Siddhaartha.'

'Which is your country?'

'Kapilavastu.'

'And your trade?'

'I am a king by trade,' Siddhaartha said. 'Or so I used to be.' Never before had they seen wayfaring kings; they conferred among themselves awhile, and then confronted the stranger again.

'King,' the citizens' leader said, 'tell us if you honour the ideology of the Celestial Birds.'

'You must pardon me,' Siddhaartha said, bewildered; he had travelled far over the mountains, and far across time, and yet, he now realized, he had much to learn. He smiled, and did not say any more. The citizens conferred, and their leader spoke to them, 'We have to know the truth. Let us bring him to the test.'

The leader hit Siddhaartha, and winced when his own fist hurt. He drew back, and watched in dismay as the blood cleared away from the stranger's mouth and the face lit up again. Siddhaartha smiled. The man hit him a second time, and still Siddhaartha smiled. In a gathering terror of incomprehension the citizens fell on the King, belabouring him, when suddenly the tavern keeper called out, 'Sacrament!'

It was after sundown, the Hour of the Second Defecation. The anthem played over the radio. Immediately the citizens abandoned the stranger, and turned towards the music. They sang. Their eyes welled with tears, and soon they were swaying as one, from side to side, mesmerized. Siddhaartha sat on a while longer, and no one noticed him any more. No one stopped him as he left the tavern.

A breeze blew in from the trees and the unpeopled spaces of the dusk. The King walked away.

CHAPTER III

The General

During the Great Decolonization, the departing Imperialisms had bequeathed costume kits and obsolete weapons to their freed colonies: there were interminable parades in all the new republics, which could devise no better use for their new-found sovereignties. In Dharmapuri there was a parade every month. Weapons were taken out of silos and towed along, the people saw the heraldic emblems and the shine of metal and rejoiced. The weapons were antique, but so were Dharmapuri's wars, antique wars waged on antique neighbours. Much of the weaponry bore White Confederate patents and were obsolete by a century: ironclads, and flying machines so primitive that one fancied they nested, and explosive devices that raised palls of stench and dust. But Dharmapuri had no military budget, only a budget for Sorrowing and Persuading, and so became the most pacific nation on earth.

Scholars streamed in from the White Confederacy to study the ancient military artifacts. Cryptologists and antiquaries found Dharmapuri an inexhaustible treasure-house, but the government severely screened their inflow. The scrutinies and obstacles were so numerous that most of the scholars went back; and for those who eventually made it to the armouries the shock of witnessing their own baroque past was often the cause of neurotic indisposition. There were also occasions, not infrequent, when a spy of the Confederacy was caught pilfering Dharmapuri's military secrets, his embarrassment all the greater because this was intelligence concerning his own obsolete weapons. Spy scares would then convulse Dharmapuri, and since it was not possible to hold white spies in captivity or punish them, native proxies were caught and executed.

Despite the silos and the guards, metal inexorably aged and tired; then the damp and vapours of the deep earth would set to work on it, and often the armourers would find a whole generation of weapons in a state of terminal rust. These weapons the President would sell to lesser presidents, the ones ruling over tiny islands of history, marooned oligarchs content to maul their subjects and one another with rust.

Dharmapuri's armouries were replenished regularly by the White Confederacy, and at the monthly ceremonials the President would reassure the people of his powers of persuasion. The Confederate Navy itself was to have a taste of this, when one of its aircraft carriers cruised into Dharmapuri's territorial waters. Dharmapuri had its own warship; a vessel salvaged and welded together in the Empire's workhouses and set afloat to mark the country's Independence. This vessel went out to meet the intruder. The Confederate carrier was driven by nuclear power, and in ring upon ring round the awesome crustacean were submarines, missile launchers, destroyers, frigates and cruisers. None of these stopped Dharmapuri's vessel as she skimmed past and headed for the mother vessel. The carrier's crew crowded onto the deck for a closer view of this strange man of war: they could identify it with nothing they had learned about at the Naval Academy. It drew astern; the Confederate sailors had a clear view of the craft now, yet fed as they were on legends of Eastern seas, the fear of the absurd and the ancient persisted. The antique pressed home her advantage: her spindly Admiral, tottering under the weight of his decorations, appeared at the prow, and accosted the Confederates in the name of the Celestial Birds. It is said that the fear of Eastern sea-sorcery came over the Confederates, and they pulled back to the high seas.

As credible is another version which has it that Dharmapuri's seamen, when they got close to the carrier, took out their empty mess cans, and holding them out to the Confederates, set up a chorus, *We are not alone, the Tartar Republic is with us!* whereupon a Tartar submarine surfaced and began signalling requests for a popular brand of Confederate cola. Overcome by traditional Imperialist guilt, the carrier and its ensemble retreated.

*

Imperialism had its presence in Shantigrama in the form of the Confederate trading houses; these fortress-like structures caused the citizens, as they passed them, to rage and smoulder. However, the Imperialists had their uses: as many as fourteen members of the President's family, sons and sons-in-law, held ceremonial vice-presidencies in these establishments. The common citizens saw this as their country's hegemony over Imperialism. These fourteen, spoilt children of people's power, had not found time in their youth to master letters, and were even worse at reckoning, but were much praised by *Prava* as leaders of the new decolonized cultures. The Confederates, on their part, kept the fourteen in comfort, giving them gleaming limousines to travel in, big blonde women attendants, and stocks of aphrodisiacs and striped candy. Their wives were prolific mothers, a condition encouraged in no small measure by the aphrodisiacs; and the President was well pleased with the rising numbers of the dynasty. On his numerous state visits abroad he took his enormous brood with him, and they descended on their hapless hosts with the harrowing thoroughness of an invasion.

Dharmapuri's scholars of current history have recorded and elaborately commented upon one such event, the Confederate banquet for the visiting President. The dynasty by then numbered a hundred and fifty. And its members, in defiance of the hypocrisies of protocol, waylaid the stewards even before the banquet had formally begun, and seized the food with whoops of delight. The Great White Father sat back, looking on in wonder at their militant appetites. As the chase for food got under way, one of the presidential offspring shat in the excitement of pursuit and circled the banquet table with a trail of slime. Then another one shat, and yet another; soon the whole brood followed suit. Their indulgent grandsire, meanwhile, fed avidly on a steak, until unable to hold it inside him, he opened his sluices as well; presently he was sitting on a sumptuous cushion of excrement, and seated thus, he addressed his host, 'White Excellency! We have our differences, but have much in common as well,' a private truth to which, in the compelling presence of excrement, the Great White Father hastily assented. The dynasty was now wallowing in dung with much clatter and unsettling of crockery; the patriarch chided them for interrupting the palaver of presidents.

Food and wine are great equalizers, and the euphoria of banquets has often encouraged the poorest of the earth's rulers to stand up to imperial powers; it is thus that the diplomatic services of decolonized countries have become dominated by bartenders and chefs. Now, sunk deep in food, wine and excrement, Dharmapuri's President went on to assert that of their two countries his was the richer in tradition and wisdom. The Great White Father was used to such brag from the tiny presidents and midget emperors who ate at his table, and would never dispute their claims even while choosing one of their countries for carpet bombing. He would tell his prospective victim, with much bowing and clinking of glasses, *It is true, Your Tiny Excellency, the New World has a good deal to learn from your ancient civilization.*

'Brown Excellency,' the Great White Father said, 'we have indeed heard much about your Celestial Birds.'

Satisfied, Dharmapuri's President and his entourage now gorged on the desserts, and in an attempt to undo the past wrongs of plundering Imperialisms, hunted among the gold and silverware for souvenirs.

*

The President often worried about his progeny; like a mollusc

21

hiding its jelly inside a giant conch, he wonld sit in the lonely gloom of the palace, while outside the shell roared a dark sea of clangorous absurdity—his past with its shame of pimping and vagrancy, demagogy and terrorism, and the frenetic pursuit of food. He would see the sea lash his children and consume them; fear would grow and become a colic within, causing him to excrete at unexpected times and in improbable places, in the armoury and into the arms of his scented concubines. These aberrations would last for days and paralyse the affairs of state. During one such interlude, the President lay prostrate, naked save for the nation's colours tied across his genitals. Around his couch, in a reverential circle, stood his cabinet; the Ministers sensed in their Lord one of his periodic seizures of fear. The President asked, 'What will happen if we are forced to go to the polls and the Convention of the Holy Spirit is beaten?' The Ministers made elaborate pretence of consulting learned tomes, and answered variously, *The ideology of the Celestial Birds will be endangered; Dharmapuri will no longer be able to lead the struggle for peace; mankind will become spiritually leaderless; there will be no one to prevent a nuclear holocaust.*

The President rose in a rage, and flinging away the nation's colours, said 'Speak straight, devious vermin!' The Ministers wet their bark and stammered, 'Mercy, sire. We shall, if Your Grace will pardon us.' They grovelled before him and the oldest among them spoke, 'The Confederate warehouses will take back the limousines and the blonde women from the Young Excellencies and withhold the supplies of candy.'

A great terror seized the President then, and he howled, 'O they will sack my children, they will sack them all!' and the Council of Ministers joined in the lament. He paced back and forth, and from his behind syringed the steaming hieroglyphs of his anger. When he had done with this preface, he stood tense, and the Ministers, trembling, told one another, 'A Proclamation, it is a Proclamation!' The President bent forward and crowed, and out came a turd as big as a sewer rat; and with that was promulgated what came to be known as the State of Crisis.

The news was broadcast and printed that the country was beseiged by the Enemy, and that neither the seas nor the mountains were defence enough. Shantigrama's citizens listened to the sound of gunfire in the night and to the wailing of sirens, they saw the glow of distant fires, and spoke in terrified whispers of the enemy within. 'My beloved people,' the President said in a midnight broadcast, 'give me your freedoms, henceforth let them be hidden inside me, because it is to rob you of thesinsidious enemy has penetrated us.' The people were grateful to be sry citizen, now and again, settling with wasp's feet on his earfor a brief while, before winging away to the next defenceless host. But the people easily overcame these feeble disturbances. *No,* they told themselves, *not the President, the Supreme Commander of the Congregation of Persuaders; never would he imprison and torture his own subjects!* The Palace brought out colourful stamps of the President squatting among heaps of carrot and lettuce, munching on the vegetables, and defecating—a picture of deep and enduring peace which reinforced the people's faith in their pacific Presidency. There was praise all round for the President's resilience and courage, but the most articulate endorsement came from *Prava* which said, 'Dharmapuri has done away with the last obstacle which Imperialism had left in the way of liberation, the Law of Habeas Corpus. Now Dharmapuri joins those who march in the grand parade of human progress.' The Communards of Dharmapuri welcomed these abridgements of rights with a fervour that dismayed even the Partisans of the Holy Spirit; often welcoming their own imprisonment, the Communards recalled the Great Tartar Purges and rejoiced in the comparison.

*

The Crisis had come to stay, gently fearsome and familiar like the tiger in the neighbourhood zoo. But soon the President became despondent again, and he lamented to the Ministers who stood round his couch, 'We promised the people a Sorrow, we promised them an enemy, and time is running out...'

And so the news was broken to the people that a Confederate armada had set sail for Dharmapuri and would soon disgorge machines of war on its shores. The Tartar Radio promptly announced a ballet festival to defend Dharmapuri. The White Confederacy was embarrassed and weakly denied it was invading anyone, blaming the impression on the noisiness and brashness of its tourists. That convinced nobody in Dharmapuri and the streets resounded again with slogans against Imperialism. Within seven days of the newsbreak the trading houses raised the wages of the presidential offspring five-fold. This was construed as a debacle for Imperialism, and greeted with riotous rejoicing in Shantigrama. Soon two giant Confederate freighters came ashore and unloaded their cargo under cover of night. It was wheat, red wheat fed to cattle in the Confederate ranches and to humans in Dharmapuri. There were also crates of sweetened feed and candy for the Palace and for the Ministers. The ships slunk away as they had come, in the night. As the days went by, the armada became tiny ships of the mind, their little sirens softly pierced the dreams of men; and the Great Crisis, the old zoo tiger, the gentle evil, stayed on.

This was the state of Dharmapuri when Siddhaartha arrived.

*

A parade was on in Shantigrama, and Siddhaartha threaded his way to the rim of the crowd to watch. As he did so, a doggerel from his childhood came to him:

Ka twam baale? Kaanchanamaala.
Kasyaa putree? Kanakalataaya.
Kim te haste? Taalee patram.
Kaavaa rekha? Ka Kha Ga Gha!

The crowd seethed and swirled, then slept within itself, like silt on the river bank, and between the banks the march rolled away bearing the delusions of the freed slave. Chariot followed chariot, formation followed formation. Each ironclad was worth

24

a million pieces of gold, all that gold merely to carry one soldier in duel against another! Surely they could have wrestled instead, thought Siddhaartha, or gambled, tossed or slanged; ways of contention as senseless, but which hurt little and wasted even less. *It passes my understanding,* the King said to himself in despair, *I am the dull-witted one.* Those who had their wits about them made the wars, they spent the substance of men age after age, and strewed fields of battle with the dismembered dead.

Once long ago a distraught god had stood between embattled armies and sought in vain to unravel the riddle of the killing and the dying. Siddhaartha did not desire to recall the *Gita,* the song of the god, but only the doggerel of his childhood. A darkness seemed to gather beyond the reaches of the march, and there the dead of the wars lay scattered; in this darkness the little girl of the doggerel stood gazing upon Siddhaartha.

Who are you, little one? asked Siddhaartha.

I am Kaanchanamaala, she said *Kanakalata's daughter.*

What do you hold in your hand?

Palm leaves, sir.

And what have you written on them?

Oh, it is the Ka *and the* Kha, *the* Ga *and the* Gha!

Between the armies of the darkness Siddhaartha heard only this doggerel, and the little girl of the doggerel and they communed with each other, telling of the *Ka* and the *Kha* the *Ga* and the *Gha,* the mysterious seals of childhood. Now she was moving away; Siddhaartha called after her, but she had disappeared in the distance where the darkness loomed heavy.

Siddhaartha turned once again to the march. As a soldier passed by, his chest covered with medals, he said 'Soldier, that is a heavy burden of war you carry.'

Someone tapped Siddhaartha on the back; it was a Partisan of the Holy Spirit.

'Soldier, did you say?' the Partisan demanded.

'Your pardon, sir,' Siddhaartha said. 'Did I say anything wrong?'

'Plenty. That was not a *soldier*, but a *Persuader*. This is a Congregation of Persuaders. Of these you seem to have no knowledge. I presume you are an alien?'

'I come from far away.'

'Which is your country?'

Alas, thought Siddhaartha, they asked that of every wayfarer, in the facile camaraderie of the road; but in him the question only awakened a penitence for the guilt of kings and wars. He had left Kapilavastu to atone for these inventions of men.

Siddhaartha answered, 'Country, sir? I have none.'

'What deprivation!' the Partisan said.

'I was in a strange trade, sir,' Siddhaartha said, 'where they asked such questions ever so often it clouded my mind, and I began this journey of mine.'

'What trade was it?'

'Sir,' said Siddhaartha with some trepidation, 'I worked at being King.'

'You are sick,' the Partisan said. 'Come with me, and let me make you whole.'

Siddhaartha willed that the Partisan should not see him; unseen, he moved along the great pathway, and soon the Partisan was gone. Suddenly there was cheering and clapping; Siddhaartha saw a picturesque chariot approach in a blaze of brass and clatter of shafts and cranks. On its high perch sat Paraashara, Dharmapuri's General, holding a jewelled turd in his hand. Siddhaartha laughed. Not at the jewelled turd, but at the medals spangling the commander's chest, the imbecile residue of war. Siddhaartha was amused that grown men should lend themselves to such comedy.

'General, Excellency!' Siddhaartha called out, softly and joyfully, and laughed some more. Like a mantis sporting enormous spiked headgear, the General turned his head, seeking out the source of the laughter. Siddhaartha laughed out loud now, without ridicule, and with abundant pity. Soon the laughter enveloped the march and choked the chariot; the laughter grew and stretched, it became a swamp through which the ironclad plodded.

Now there was nothing but the swamp; the General sat on his perch and wailed, 'Where are you, laughing stranger?' There was no answer, only the great baptism of that laughter, until he could bear it no more. He leapt down from the chariot, and as he stood there enveloped by the laughter, the chariot too was lost to view. In the dense wet colours of earth and leaf that sought rebirth in decaying, the swamp stretched without end. Paraashara sank and floundered, and blindly sought his way ...Siddhaartha, laughing no more, watched the march again, and again Kaanchanamaala beckoned.

Look at my eyes, my King, said Kaanchanamaala.

Merciful Lord! said Siddhaartha. *I see dead orbs, white and sightless like sparrows' eggs!*

While I slept in my mother's womb, said Kaanchanamaala, *no one fed my little eyes. They fed their wars instead, and I came sightless into this world.*

My little one, O my little one, said Siddhaartha.

Look at my palm leaves, my King, said Kaanchanamaala. *I never wrote on them.*

Siddhaartha leaned forward, and for a moment held her palm in his, but she dissolved like the mist of the night, moving once again towards her dead.

*

The General ran on, unseeing, ploughing through people. His sodden clothes flapped about him like wings. In this state he reached his mother's door, and called out to her.

'My son!' answered a grating voice from inside and the door opened. A wizened old woman looked out. Paraashara brushed past her and ran towards the inner chambers, trailing a line of slime. His mother wept when she saw her son's disarray.

'Ah, my little son,' she sobbed, as the maids came in with mops,'someone has tormented my little son!'

'Whoever has vexed His Excellency,' the maids said, 'will be punished, O Mother of the Congregation of Persuaders!'

*

In the room where he had spent his boyhood, playing with hoppers and ladybirds, a great boyhood joy returned to Paraashara. In the joy of play, he plucked off his medals one by one, medals from which the scent of blood had gone and which were now like the playthings of a child; he cast them away without hate, like a child does his toys. Next he peeled away his general's costume and stood naked before the mirror. Silently the maids tiptoed into the chamber, while the old woman kept anxious vigil outside.

There was a knock at the outer door, and Paraashara's mother, opening it, found a delegation of colonels drawn up in the patio. On seeing her the colonels prostrated themselves before her, grovelling on the cobbles. Then rising, the oldest among them addressed her, 'Venerable Mother of the Congregation of Persuaders! His Excellency fled the parade, but his scent led us here. This flight might well unsettle the Presidential Defecation, dampen the struggle of the subject peoples and cause Imperialism to rejoice. I had foreseen this in the dissertation I wrote for the Patrose Lecomba Tartar University. I have brought the dissertation along, and it should convince His Excellency that he must rejoin this evening's finale.'

Paraashara's mother called out, 'O my son, your colonel awaits your pleasure. He has brought his dissertation along.'

'Your Excellency ...' began the colonel.

In deep peace Paraashara replied from inside, 'Go away, brethren!'

The stench of excrement was gone from his body. Gone too was the evil of war, and he laughed like the stranger. And like that precious find of his childhood, the caterpillar, he slid over the maids in larval gratitude, while from outside, once again, the distraught colonel tried to remind him of the threat from Imperialism.

CHAPTER IV

The Kitchen Maid

The parade concluded without the General, the President and his Ministers, in distress, went into retreat. When Rumannuaan, the Minister for Sorrowing, reached home, he tiptoed into the kitchen and took hold of the breasts of Laavannya the kitchen maid. When he did this, she did not flinch, but a heavy day had tired her, so in the faint hope of dissuading him, she spoke gently, 'My Lord, the subject peoples of the Black and Brown continents demand your attention. Must you waste it on these trivial nipples of mine?'

'O Laavannya,' Rumannuaan said, 'dark forces stalk the country, and have spirited our Commander away.'

'Alas!' Laavannya said.

As Rumannuaan wound himself tighter round the kitchen maid, he creaked like the rusted weapons of Dharmapuri, for his works of bone and spike and cartilage had long grown brittle inside their wrapping of parchment. Her garments gave way and her breasts came into view. Rumannuaan grinned at the sight. He slavered over her. From the crevices between his teeth, where smatterings of the Sacrament remained, came a pestilential stench. As it swept over her, Laavannya blanched and Rumannuaan, seeing this pallor, asked,'Fair one, I see that you are preoccupied. What are you thinking about?'

'The threat to the Celestial Birds, sire,' she replied.

'A timely concern indeed, because Imperialism today is making surreptitious assaults on their ideology.'

The Minister for Sorrowing tightened his fingers on her breasts, and Laavannya, overwhelmed by the stench, said distractedly, 'May Your Grace be pleased to free my nipples, because freedom is the recognition of necessity, as Friedrich Engels has wisely said.'

Her confusion grew when she realized that she had quoted a classic saying out of context, but Rumannuaan appeared not to notice. He said 'Well said, O tormentor of my loins! We hold Engels in great esteem. As indeed we do his dependent, Karl Marx, the *Tribune's* former correspondent in London, an excellent newsman who has greatly contributed to our resistance to Imperialism. But in insisting that your breasts be freed, you act without awareness of the Great Crisis.'

It was but a mild admonition, but it reminded Laavannya of the danger she was in; were she to be imprudent about her breasts, she could be inviting the charge of criminal dissidence. So before she made her next move to loosen his hold on them, she took refuge in the protective incantation, *The Incomparable Sacrament be praised!* As she sought to prise the gnarled fingers loose, she marvelled at their strength. *The strength of Feringhee feed,* surmised Laavannya: for Rumannuaan had spent his youth in Feringheeland, snake-charming and selling trinkets, and propagating the cause of Dharmapuri's independence; he charmed ageing countesses as well, and they fed him during all those years in Feringheeland.

Rumannuaan gripped her breasts tighter; she made the ritual chant, *We are not alone, the Tartar Republic is with us!* hoping, foolishly, to embarrass the Minister. When that ploy failed, she swore to herself in despair: *Old lecher, carcass-eater, people of my class seldom live beyond fifty; I am thirty-five, which leaves me another fifteen years in which to let my blood thin and my fats clot and my skin turn to parchment. Carcass-eater, the maggots are inside you, but with the rarest physic you keep your lust alive. God, God, I want to live not just those fifteen years, but beyond them; I want to cross over with my breasts and behind firm and my mouth fragrant. I want to love, love, in my fragrant eventide and bleed for the seeds of men.*

The old man's slaver fell on her neck and shoulders; his fingers crawled over knots and buttons like slow-jointed spiders, and clumsily but surely went on undressing her. Then he blew his conch calling forth officers of the Congregation of Persuaders, who undid the last of her tenacious undergarments and made an inventory of her clothes. (The armed forces always taught one to make inventories.) Laavannya thought fast: how best to ward off the death-stench at least for this evening?

'My Lord,' she said, 'you spoke once at the Assembly of Nations for seven hours without pause. For seven persistent hours you kept the Imperialists at bay. My Lord, I desire to hear you deliver that speech again.'

This ploy failed too; the old man, with single-minded purpose, lay down on the kitchen floor and positioned the stripped maid above him. She could feel the cadaverous mouth move beneath her. *God, God,* she thought, fascinated, *here I crush with my flesh so much wealth of history!* as under her, his mouth smothered by her buttocks, lay the intrepid revolutionary whose words even the might of empires could not stop. *The buttock smothers more decisively,* thought Laavannya, contemplating the weapons that were still available to her class. Seated thus, she set off on a comparative assessment of Marx and Freud and Skinner, and inferred the prime lesson that Man cannot be *predicted.* Now from beneath her buttocks, in bursts of whistling breath, came the voice of the Third World radical, 'Sumptuous daughter of Dharmapuri! Your posterior relegates to insignificance the behinds of Feringhee countesses!'

'My Lord,' Laavannya said, 'your generous words place me in heavy debt. How can I repay it?'

'Easily done,' the voice from beneath her buttocks said, 'with a little excrement.'

'Mine?' Laavannya said, aghast. 'My Lord, you must be sorely distracted to accord to my excrement the adoration due to the Presidential Host. Should this desire of yours be fulfilled, we would be committing treason. Already you have grossly erred by making goat noises while disrobing me. No one save the President (and the goats, of course, who know no protocol) is allowed to make these noises. No, my Lord, no!'

Rumannuaan concentrated on Laavannya's buttocks so intensely in his anticipation of excrement, that he lost his grip on the rest of her anatomy; Laavannya wriggled free, with no illusion of escape but merely a woman's instinctual sense of resistance. The old man rose now, and removing his clothes for freer movement, chased her round the spacious imperial kitchen. Back again in his grip, and pinioned to the floor, Laavannya began working fast on other strategems.

'Our gracious mistress,' she said, 'your beloved wife...'

This was a desperate gambit, but Rumannuaan only laughed.

'Have no fear. She will not come upon us, because today the President has her.'

Rumannuaan's wife was a woman of great beauty, and younger than him by half-a-century. For a moment Laavannya forgot her own nakedness and captivity.

'Merciful God!' she said. 'Do you masters have to do *this* as well? I had supposed it was enough to partake of the Sacrament.'

Rumannuaan's face fell, and so did his vital member, and Laavannya said to herself, *Ah, so this man too experiences sadness!* The sharing of sadness was the virtue of her class; she could do so even with those that came to take her as they would a whore; it was in such sadness that she began stroking the Minister's feeble sex.

'One wishes one could stop with the Sacrament,' Rumannuaan said cheerlessly. 'But it does not suffice, O my kitchen maid! One has to part with one's woman too. Such is the awesome process of history.'

'But we're we not taught that history is the struggle of classes?'

Rumannuaan grew silent and more morose, whereupon Laavannya continued, 'My Lord, if such be the substance of history, let us repudiate history.'

For Rumannuaan, in that moment of discomfort, history resolved itself as his power over the kitchen maid, and hence the disowning of it aroused great anxieties in him; Laavannya felt the sweat break out over his naked body.

'No!' Rumannuaan said. 'Were there no history, what will become of nations, and without nations what will become of frontiers, and without frontiers where will your Persuader-husband stand guard?'

If there were no history, the kitchen maid wondered, *on which snowy desolation would my husband need to stand guard and be shot down? This old man with the slavering mouth will never be shot down!* In the virgin anger of her class, she cursed the genitals of the old man and the likes of him who could make men shoot and be shot down. The next instant, however, she was stricken by remorse; *God* she prayed, *let not my curse come true, and let no one be so afflicted, but cause love to flow like river floods through men, even the enemies of my class.* No longer did she try to free herself; she saw the struggle of the subject peoples and the triumph of statesmen shrink into the space of a kitchen and the triviality of an incompetent act of lust; the body of love decayed, and from it rose the stench of its slavering mouth.

'Were there no history,' Laavannya said, 'who then would pimp wives away?'

Laavannya had said it in sadness rather than in derision, but it hit the old man like a harpoon; Rumannuaan's eyes overflowed, and Laavannya, mopping up the tears with kisses in a surge of pity, said, 'My poor Master! I never meant to cause you distress. Do not cry. I shall not remind you of anything, but arouse you instead with gentle inducement. Come, my Lord, lie still.'

Rumannuaan lay on the kitchen floor, and straddling him Laavannya futilely nursed his limpness. Presently Rumannuaan stopped crying, and grabbed his conch and blew it, calling forth his officers, who, on a sign from him, fetched vials of Tartar and Confederate potions, and a native aphrodisiac as well; they began administering these to the Minister. At the end of an hour's ministration Rumannuaan's passion rose, and he mounted the kitchen maid. Laavannya acknowledged the efficacy of the Tartar and Confederate potions, but was reassured that the native physic had worked as well. She was glad that

Dharmapuri had taken great strides in this most intricate of pharmacologies. Since Rumannuaan's strokes were feeble despite the potions, Laavannya took the opportunity to recall without interruption the voluminous body of statistics and editorial commentary on the subject. While she was thus engaged, Rumannuaan, unknown to her emitted weakly, and grew quiet. It was some time before she became aware of the stillness of the old man who lay on her, and she said, 'My Lord, pardon me if I failed you as a citizen by not participating in your magnificent ejaculation. I was engrossed in statistics and commentary on the state of indigenous technology.'

'Most laudable! It bespeaks your commitment.'

His voice trailed away, and he lay as in a swoon; outside the kitchen it was a sombre evening. Laavannya slipped out from under the old man and walked out of the kitchen and across the lobbies and down the corridors, until she reached the Minister's personal secretariat. To the officer who sat there she said, 'Kapitan, be pleased to give me back my clothes.'

'I specialize in mountain sorrowfare,' the officer said. 'My monograph on the subject is a standard reference work. I presume you have read it?'

'I have no reason to doubt the work is significant. I must admit, though, that I have not had the occasion to read it.'

'At least some of the reviews?'

Laavannya now became desperate. 'Not the reviews, either,' she said.'My clothes, there right behind you...'

The officer turned round, and rummaging among her clothes, ferreted out the dossier of reviews.

*

Darkness had set in by the time Laavannya returned home.

'God, my gracious God!' she exclaimed, when she saw Vaatasena, her Persuader-husband, waiting for her in the patio—he had abandoned the Celestial Birds and deserted his guardsman's kiosk! What could have made him do it? she thought in anguish. Terrible was the punishment that awaited the deserter.

Vaatasena spoke to her in incoherence and anger, 'Our child lies ill with a fever.'

Laavannya rushed into the house; and the Persuader, following her, said, ominously gesturing with his hands, 'Ah, my child, my suffering child! I might as well have strangled you.'

'Sunanda! Sunanda!' said Laavannya, and covered the boy like a hen covers her chick.

'Laavannya,' Vaatasena said, lighting a lamp and gazing on her for a long while, 'I see your cheeks stained, I see them soiled by other men.'

Laavannya no longer cried for her son, but sobbed in another sorrow.

'These long and wind-blown years,' the Persuader said, 'I stood on the mountains, hungering.'

Laavannya rose, but her feet gave way. Vaatasena held her as she fell ... Suddenly a voice from the dark commanded, 'Stand apart! The kitchen maid and her Persuader-husband started. Four secret policemen stalked in, put fetters on the deserting Persuader, and hauled him to the black chariot that waited outside. The chariot moved away, and in his fever the boy cried for his father.Laavannya did not weep; her eyes glistened dry as she sat beside her son ... Then a sudden darkness enveloped her.

CHAPTER V

The Merciful Stranger

When she came to her senses, Laavannya found the black chariot gone. Down the dimly lit street she ran in blind and futile chase. The pursuit, its hopelessness, soon wearied her, and she felt faint again. When it passed, she was lying on the sidewalk, with Sunanda kneeling beside her. Feebly she stretched her hand out to feel the child's forehead.

'My child,' she said, 'you have come all this way in your fever!'

'Mother, where have they taken him?'

'My son,' she began, and stopped short, for at that instant, around them, rose a querulous flight of bats, with a great flapping of wings. As Laavannya and Sunanda looked up, a pair of burning topazes, neurotic yellow in the night, returned their gaze from within the dense canopy of a nearby tree. Sunanda shuddered.

'Have no fear, son. It is but an owl.'

But the owl spoke from the tree, 'You are mistaken. I am from the secret police.'

'Mercy!' said Laavannya in amazement and fear; the secret policeman slithered down the tree like a giant wood snake and stood before them. The bats wheeled away like images in a delirium, and were lost in the far shores of the starlight.

'What were you talking about?' the secret policeman demanded.

'About bats and owls. You must pardon us, sir.'

'That is not necessary. You have not answered my question.'

'Kapitan, my child here has fever...'

'Was that why you pursued the chariot?'

Hesitantly Laavannya replied, 'We did not pursue the chariot,

36

my Kapitan.'

'We shall find that out,' the secret policeman said. 'Follow me now.'

'Where to, my Kapitan?'

'Ask no questions.' the secret policeman said. 'There is a Crisis on.'

Laavannya and Sunanda followed the secret policeman, and presently arrived at a fortress of interrogation; their captor ordered them to enter. Getting behind his desk, and assuming the unchallengeable power men assume behind desks, he began filling in the inevitable questionnaire: her name and her husband's, his occupation and domicile, and a host of irrelevant and trivial entries, until at last, shorn of her privacy, she stood intimidated in the presence of its columns. Then the secret policeman put the paper away, and came to her with a measuring tape. 'Your breasts...'

Laavannya knew that the ways of the state were often strange in times of historical insecurity; despite this she asked, 'Is this necessary, Kapitan?'

'Absolutely,' the secret policeman said, and proceeded to measure her breasts and her buttocks. Then he prised open her mouth to count her teeth.

'The grinder there needs to be pulled out,' the secret policeman said after prolonged scrutiny, 'and this canine needs filling.'

'I suppose so.'

'Well, now the lips. Let us have a look.'

Laavannya pushed her lips out in a full, wet pout; the secret policemen immediately kissed them a number of times. Quickly in her mind, she went over the defence parameters of Dharmapuri, and, evaluating its threat perceptions, endured the kisses, but soon turned her mouth away as her lips began to smart. This caused the secret policeman to persist with renewed violence and passion. Sunanda came to his mother's defence, and in the ensuing scuffle bruised his head against a desk; Laavannya, her lips dripping with the kisses, pleaded, 'Mercy, sir! My son bleeds.' But the secret policeman was struggling to disrobe her now, growing more and more angry as she restored each undone hook and button, slipping back under cover each inch of exposed territory. Finally, exasperated beyond measure, he gave up, and ejaculated onto the floor.

'Do you realize,' he said, 'it is treason to frustrate thus a servant of the state?'

The enormity of the danger she faced became apparent to her as she sat up to set her hair and tidy her clothes: the country was in a state of seige, and no tribunal was likely to entertain a citizen's defence against an accusing Kapitan.

'Pardon my folly, sir,' Laavannya said. 'I shall no more resist a servant of the state.'

She undressed and stood, naked and dazzling, before her assailant and her son.

'Look away, my child,' she said. 'Whatever your mother is doing is for the country, and countries make demands that are often inscrutable to their citizens.'

The secret policeman tried to take her, but his efforts quickly slackened and he stood disconsolate.

'What now, my Kapitan?' Laavannya asked.

'Impudent hussy! Asking such a question! Can you not see that I have lost my power?'

Laavannya soothed him,'It could happen to the most power-ful of men. Come, my Kapitan, I shall rouse you.'

Shame drove him to a frenzy. 'Let me get this over with! Then will I take you straight to prison!'

'No, no, my Kapitan, this is no reason to be unkind to me.' Saying this she laid the secret policeman on the floor, counsel-ling her son once again to look away; Sunanda obeyed, but in fearsome persistence his gaze turned again and again towards his mother and the secret policeman. The Kapitan lay limp, in the sovereign rage of the impotent.

'All will be well,' Laavannya said, in an attempt to reassure him. 'It was but a little while ago that I roused the Minister thus...'

The secret policeman yelped. 'You roused a Minister! Which Minister?'

'The Minister for Sorrowing.'

The secret policeman went pale, shuddered, and with a moan scrambled up. In the abruptness of the disengagement he injured his member, which Laavannya had been trying to rouse with labial witchery. He stood before her, palms joined in contrition, even as she sat half-kneeling and contemplated his injury.

'Mercy!' he said to the bewildered Laavannya. 'Mercy on this miserable one!'

Meanwhile Sunanda had gathered up his mother's clothes and laid them at her feet; but Laavannya merely sat gazing at them, distracted and unseeing. The child picked them up and wound them round her breasts and navel.

'Am I free, my Kapitan?' Laavannya asked but her tormentor, now speechless with terror, could not answer her. She waited a little longer, but as he showed no sign of recovery, she rose, and with one last look at his intimate bruise, walked out of the fortress.

*

She walked dispiritedly down the street again, the ailing Sunanda beside her. Presently she came to the alley of the medicine sellers and stepped into a shop. 'My son here,' she said, 'has a fever.' From behind a counter of glittering crystals the apothecary leered at Laavannya. She felt sick and turned away, for she knew the face: this was the apothecary who had sold spurious vaccines to the orphanages and slaughtered a thousand children. In shop after shop, from behind crystal counters, leered murderous apothecaries; as she turned away from them, their laughter pursued her retreat.

'Son,' she said, 'there is no physic for us in this alley.'

They left the alley and the great pathways behind, and walked far. The darkness grew heavy. They were now on the bank of a river. *What now?* thought Laavannya as she seated her fevered son on her lap. *God, my God!* she chanted; the inheritance of many generations had taught her to pray, but anger overcame supplication, anger and hapless revolt. *No* she said, *I shall not take that Name again.*

'Mother,' the child asked, 'will I die?'

She held him close, she rose and raged inside like a smouldering pyre. Her legs gave way, and she sat down on the river bank. She did not know how long she sat thus; a gentle touch on her shoulder woke her from her grieving.

'You were crying,' said the stranger. 'What sorrow made you cry?'

Laavannya knew the stranger needed no answers, knew that he knew that in her grieving she had cursed her country and denied her God. She looked up at him mutely, and now the stranger spoke into her mind, *Do not cry over these, but find succour in what you may never have to repudiate: these trees and this river and the grace of this meeting on its banks,* and Laavannya answered his thought, *Ah, I need little else.* He laid his hand on the child's forehead, then wading into the river, scooped up a palmful of water and threw it as an offering into the night.'Living waters,' he said, 'healing skies, immortal guardians of the universe! Take unto yourselves the pain of this son!'

Laavannya's tears coursed down her cheeks.

'Who are you, merciful stranger?'

'Siddhaartha.'

'Who?'

'The King.'

CHAPTER VI

The Mendicant

All that lay behind her now, miraculously distanced: Ruman-nuaan's kitchen and the fortress of the interrogators, the slush of bodies and the crippling odours; Laavannya walked the river bank, no longer afraid, feeling the soft recuperative earth beneath her. She sorrowed for Vaatasena, and soon overcome by sorrow, lay down on the moss. Sunanda lay down beside her, and was soon asleep. Siddhaartha took the shawl off his shoulders and covered the child.

'O Siddhaartha,' Laavannya said, 'the river winds are cold and your shoulders are bare.

'Siddhaartha felt the child's forehead. 'The fever has cooled.'

Laavannya did not stretch her hand out to feel Sunanda's forehead, but knew the Stranger had healed her child; she gave herself up to the deep quiet of that trust. Siddhaartha laid her head on his lap, and said, 'Laavannya, you have spoken to me today about the lore of Dharmapuri. Who is the Ancient One you call the Mendicant?'

'The Father of our nation,' Laavannya said. 'He died long ago. The President had his ashes immersed in the seas with much ceremony. But those who read the stars say he will come back, though it is sedition to say so.'

Siddhaartha recalled the taboos of his own kingship, and said, 'Ah! Sedition indeed!' He spoke as King to citizen, sharing the secret vice of sovereign states.

'Do not ask me, O Siddhaartha,' Laavannya said in trepidation, 'why they make it sedition to recall the prophecy. I do not desire to dwell on it; too many people have discoursed with me today on the State and its mysterious ways.'

41

The day's abundant discourse smarted on her lip and breast and groin... Siddhaartha went back into the past and sought the image of the founding father of Dharmapuri, and presently saw him standing on Time's wasteland where great paths crossed. Beside him stood a native son of Dharmapuri, who had lost his war and his citizen's estate.

'It is another war that I have lost,' said the native son, 'the war of the bodies, of the genetic plasm.'

The Ancient One smiled, his ears outstretched and fragile like a mouse's. 'Endure it, my son.'

'I can endure it no more. The white alien takes my woman.'

The smile now left the Ancient One, and he said, 'There is no mercy in Creation, yet all Creation hungers for mercy. It is this hunger which turns the flesh of the animal and the green of the plant into soul.'

'Master, what do I call you? I do not yet know your name...'

'Call me Old Mendicant.'

'Oh, no,' the native son said, tenderly, 'I shall call you Mendicant Father.'

The Mendicant smiled once again, and said, 'You may.'

'Mendicant Father,' the native son said, disrobing himself,'Look at these limbs of mine, limbs my starved fathers have bequeathed to me. The large and blond conqueror fulfils my woman.'

'Yet rejoice and be exceeding glad,' the Mendicant said,'because there comes another war in which the victory will be yours, for in that war everyone wins.'

The native son stood uncomprehending, and the Mendicant said to him, 'Come, walk with me.'

The native son walked with him, and so did others, until there was a multitude. Seeing the multitude, the Mendicant spoke to them, 'The voice of God tells me that some day the people of Dharmapuri will have huts to live in, and that great forests will be in flower. My beloved people, be ready for them.'

'Teach us about that war, Mendicant Father,' the multitude cried.

'He that comes after me will teach you,' the Mendicant said. 'He will rouse the serpent that sleeps in the stems of your spines.'

'Who is he, Mendicant Father?'

'Of that I have no knowledge, I have none.'

*

The Feringhees were not defeated, they gave up their empire when the Mendicant called on them to become his adversaries in the war of no losers ... Siddhaartha turned away from the vision, and said to Laavannya, 'I see the Mendicant alive, and in prison.'

'O Siddhaartha,' Laavannya said, 'why does a great State have to lie to its citizens? Has it always been thus? My mind grows weary.'

'It was in such weariness that I stole out of my palace, leaving my Queen behind, and sat beneath a great *pipal* tree, to look beyond the weariness into myself. I looked and I saw, like the moon in a still lake-'

Laavannya held the King in her arms. 'O Siddhaartha, you saw your Queen?' Quietly she undid her garments, and when she had put them all away, she said, 'Look on me, Siddhaartha!'

Siddhaartha rose over her, his legs like *stupas;* behind him spread the dark foliage of the *kuvala* tree and behind it the hood of the night, outspread and serpent-blue. Soon Laavannya was still, spent with the loving, and a great joy in her spirit. Beside her Sunanda slept on.

'Merciful King,' she said, 'you healed my son, and now you have healed me.'

'The river and the trees and the sky healed us,' Siddhaartha said. 'May rivers no longer divide peoples, may bodies fulfil bodies.'

The wind rustled in the *kuvala* tree, and the birds of the night circled it. In the river a fish rose to blow a bubble. The night grew cold.

Laavannya said, 'Siddhaartha, give me your peace once again.'

CHAPTER VII

The Twice-born

Siddhaartha's was a weary childhood, for the child carried in his palm the mystic sign, the curse of the saviour. While the other princes played, young Siddhaartha sat gazing at this mark, and over the prattle of children listened to prophetic voices. His teachers despaired when he showed no alertness at reckoning; but he knew the constellations and their awesome ellipses. The scriptures held no surprises for him, only a desultory familiarity. When the teachers began initiating him in the lore of kingship, his own lineage, the Prince smiled back at them in bland distraction, for memories of another lineage gathered over him, memories of his own becoming, age after age.

Out of his hearing, the teachers complained among themselves, 'The Prince learns slowly. What will become of the kingdom when he ascends the throne?'

But Siddhaartha's teachers were elsewhere. The intelligences of trees and winds taught him, and from them he learned with eagerness; they taught him in the tender greens of shoots and in the space and freedom of the riverside.

When he became King, his family found him the most beautiful woman in the realm for Queen, and still the distraction did not leave him. They took him to see the frontiers of the kingdom, he saw only mountains and rivers. The generals despaired of their dull-witted King.

The longer he sat on the throne, the more sombre grew the distraction. One night he rose from his bed, and pausing for a moment to look back at his sleeping Queen, he slipped out of the palace.

Thus began his wandering through strange lands, and far

times, the quest for the Frontierless Kingdom.

He knocked on hermits' crypts and climbed precipices where lonely sentinels sat in searing penance and dissipation; but they all turned their faces away.

One day at sunset, at the end of a hard day's journeying, he came to a *pipal* tree. The plants of dusk were folding their leaves; Siddhaartha, quietened, sat down beneath the *pipal* to meditate. The *pipal*'s canopy came suddenly alive with the noise of nesting birds, and the grass below teemed with tiny creatures. Their celebrant noises rose round the King's meditation, then grew into subtle eddies, beyond hearing; the voice of the Frontierless Kingdom! The egg shell of memories, the home of the meditating embryo, cracked open; and from its splinters, in joy, in primordial curiosity, rose the resplendent twice-born.

CHAPTER VIII

Laughter Frees the Persuaders

On the outskirts of Shantigrama sprawled the Cantonment of Women, the ten thousand manless homes from which the men had been gone for years to be tied to distant mountain frontiers. The years had worn the women's endurance thin, and at last they petitioned the President. When the Palace page-boy brought him the scroll, the President was stretched naked on his back, with naked maids massaging him with precious ointments. The President asked a maid to read him the petition. She picked up the scroll and glanced through it; *Beloved President*, she began, then overcome with embarrassment, stopped reading.

'Read!' the President ordered.

'Sire,' the maid said, 'it is immodest.'

'Then it has come at a most opportune hour.'

The opportune hour was a joint deployment of Tartar and Confederate aphrodisiacs on the President; for well over an hour the President's genitals had been massaged with these, although to the mortification of the donor ambassadors, watching from the wings, the President's organ had not arisen. All affairs of state had been suspended, and the Communards, in ritual alarm, ran berserk on spy-hunts.

'Read!' the President ordered again, and now the maid complied.

Beloved President, she read, *the moon grows and dwindles, and clouds nest in our pubises; grinding thigh against thigh we fulfil ourselves, while our men waste away on the frontiers. The moon has waxed and waned a full twelve years; like snowy mountains colliding, our thighs produce a cold and infernal fire...*

'Read it again,' the President ordered; the maid began again, and the President's senses quickened as he listened avidly to every word; *thighs,* thought the President, *twenty thousand of them!* He interrupted the reading with stage-directions: the maid's voice grew huskier as she slid from syllable to syllable, and her moist eyes wandered over the thighs of the harem. She read on and on, now back and forth, and as thus the reading proceeded, the President began making the goat noises which the renowned Tartar orientalist Barbakov had studied for a decade. And the recital, with its lip-slosh and flapping of thighs, permeated the mix of aphrodisiacs, and the ambassadors who had waited so long in anguish, saw the President's tool rise to miraculous power.

*

In a lonely frontier outpost stood two Persuaders, and peered through spy glasses into the Hun encampment pitched across the valley.

'Aryadatta,' Ghrini, a boy barely out of his teens, said to his much older companion, 'I cannot bear to lose sight of that Hun girl-soldier. In my mind, I have taken her to a faraway seaside and undressed her over and over again.'

'I could get you punished for this,' Aryadatta said. 'She is the Enemy.'

'Ah, she is gone!'

Ghrini put away his spy glass.

Aryadatta caressed the boy's cheeks, and gently admonished him, 'Get a hold on yourself. Remember our Hun Sorrows.'

'I remember. But it is not what you might remember. O Arya-datta, it is bitter memory.'

*

The Hun wars conjured up a disconcerting image in Ghrini's

mind: a tradesman's mansion, the most splendrous in Shanti-grama. In this mansion, with its priceless carpets, its crystal and gold, and beautiful concubines picked from distant continents, lived his uncle the gun merchant. He made a billion pieces of gold in the month the Sorrow lasted. *How unfair that it lasted a mere month,* thought the concubines angrily, *Ah, if only it had gone on! Do the ragtag scum consider their lives too precious to sacrifice for the country, do they hold themselves dearer than a billion pieces of gold a month?* Ghrini recalled his uncle strok-ing his concubines' breasts and behinds, and telling them, *Be consoled, fair mistresses: there is gold in more things than war.* And indeed there was, in floods, in famine, and in the Great Plague.

'Aryadatta,' Ghrini said, 'we stand guard over the concubines!'

'It is the mountain sickness,' Aryadatta replied. 'You are losing your reason.'

A pall of mist lifted, and on the peaks the sun glistened silver. Ghrini contemplated the mountain, ageless, mighty and serene, its rivers carrying the cold sun to the valley. This was the moun-tain he held with his puny weapon! *O King of Motionless Beings!* Ghrini said in penitence, *great is my folly and my arrogance.* The mountain swelled out of the joyful earth and filled the soldier with the peace of forgiveness.

Now Ghrini heard susurròus ripples, subtle waters of an unseen lake lapping at the slopes of the mountain. They became a baptismal laugh, full of pity for the desolate sentinel.

Ghrini laid down his weapon. The palms of his hands, as he spread them in freedom, were the wings of the mountain bird, and on his lips was the smile of virgin goddesses. Aryadatta kissed those lips, and led Ghrini into the tent; the sun was bright and cold, and love filled the gorges of the snow... When they came out of the tent again, the shadows of sunset had spread over the Hun encampment. Ghrini stood for a while looking across the valley, taking leave of the Hun with slit eyes and little breasts, then took both his and Aryadatta's weapons and flung them into the gorge below; the ripples of the unseen lake closed over the artifacts of war. The ripples were now within them, a great commandment of peace; the Persuaders looked deep into each other's eyes, and smiled, they held hands and began their climb down to the plains, and to their distant homes.

*

In the cantonment, the Persuaders' wives made love to the memories of their men, to fragile and elusive images... In one of the homes of the cantonment, Mandakini, the wife of Aryadatta, sat in bed with her friend Sreelata, counselling and comforting her. Sreelata said bitterly, 'It is no use any more! The State of Dharmapuri has accomplished the ultimate divestment of its citizens. It has kept my Persuader-husband away so long that I cannot put together his image any more.'

She began to cry, and Mandakini bent over her and kissed away her tears; then she kissed her on the lips. Neither woman knew how long the kiss lasted... And in such wise were quenched the rest of the ten thousand Persuaders' wives.

These grim and sapphic tidings, as we've seen, reached the Palace; they tormented the President with visions of incensed Persuaders rising and seizing power, putting an end to the candy and the aphrodisiacs and the broad-bottomed concubines, and scattering his dispossessed children into vagrancy. The Palace Psychiatrist reassured the President and told him his fears were groundless; he had concluded, through much scholarly analysis, that the Persuaders would be enraged only if their wives sought other men. Their wives' sapphic love would merely cause them to lust in their bunkers and trenches. The President gratefully loosened his fears into the can.

Yet, beyond sapphic fulfilment, the wives dreamt of wilder loves; Mandakini and Sreelata, as they slept together, dreamed together, and in their dreams they petitioned the Enemy: *Sensuous Invader! Miscegenator of History! Our Presidency has promised us invasions time and again, but the promise has not*

49

been kept. All we have got is a decrepit state of seige which only Prava *supports. Our men, idle on the frontiers, waste their seed away. Invade us....* Tumult filled their dreams, the fire and clangour of weapons; the dreaming women opened the frontiers for the invader, they opened their flowers of lust.

*

Ghrini and Aryadatta reached the Cantonment, and walked past homes from which the fragile images of the Congregation of Persuaders had fled; the scent of woman and woman together hung in the moonlight like ancient incense. The deserting soldiers found Mandakini and Sreelata in bed, asleep in deep embrace. They stood for a long time, lost in the beautiful spectacle.

Around them the subtle laughter rose again, and the Persuaders listened; it cleansed them of jealous hurts, and the women awoke to loving and celebration.

CHAPTER IX

The Tartar Republic and the Eucharist

The Communards of Dharmapuri had not fallen for the Sacrament like the rest of the people; the Red Tartar Republic was with them. They practised the ancient regimen of historical and dialectical sorcery, and its arcane texts gave them glimpses of what went on beneath the surface of things. They pitied the people who, with no such aid, plodded through history, reading its surface graffiti and perishing in tragic summations; these were the people the Communards were eventually destined to liberate.

Or so the Tartar Republic assured them. This was again a matter in which the Communards pitied the rest of the people: no one save they had access to so infallible a sorcery, or had a global teacher to interpret it constantly. Communard historians have recorded the triumph of the arcana during the Great Floods of Dharmapuri, when the Party of the Communards, on the strength of what the Red Tartar Teacher had revealed to them, dissuaded the people from climbing into rescue craft.

'We have to look beyond the gross reality of the present,' declaimed the Communards. 'We have to defend the Tartar Motherland against Imperialist encirclement.'

'What do we do?' asked the villagers of Dharmapuri, terrified of the rising flood waters.

'Fight the Tartar drought. Leave these floods to our lumpen nationalists.'

The villagers lost hold of the boats and sank, and the Communards cheered them with much passion and solidarity as they went down. The arcana also taught the Communards criticism and self-criticism, and soon enough, through this most amazing facility, they changed their political line to one of Struggle against Superfluous Water. It was no coincidence that by then the Tartar rivers were in spate, though in Dharmapuri itself a severe drought had set in. The Communards reasoned with the villagers on the need for a popular front against floods, international floods; it was difficult reasoning, because on the parched commons the villagers' dead cattle lay unburied. The incensed villagers booed and stoned the dialectical sorcerers, who with arcane knowledge saw what others did not see; the infallible sorcery turned humiliation into secret triumph.

Then the Communards decided to seize power; the arcana assured them the objective situation was ripe. With dialecticians in command and simple aids to violence as weapons, the insurrection lasted a week, at the end of which the sorcerers were in prison. Annoyed by this, the Tartar Republic withheld from the Communards the customary Subsidy for Historical Change, and barred them from international Peace-and-Youth soup kitchens. The Communards thereupon set up a great lament in their prisons; soon the lament reached the Great Red Father who relented and sent them a secret command through a courier. Before the courier could reach Dharmapuri, the Committee of the Insurrection (which had gone underground and evaded arrest) decided to trek to the Tartar Republic. For days they trekked over inhospitable terrain, fording rapids, and crossing perilous mountain passes, until finally they stepped on Tartar earth. Smearing the soil on their foreheads in veneration, they spoke aloud in thanksgiving, 'Tartarland, Red Mother! Here we come, your international sons. Give us your big tits, suckle us!'

Speaking thus, they sat down to meditate on those life-giving tits, with eyes closed in prayer. The Chairman of the Committee was roused by a truncheon blow to the head, and he opened his eyes with the protective incantation, *We are not alone, the Tartar Republic is with us!* Standing before him was a truncheon-wielding Commissar.

'White Comrade, Comrade-sir!' the Chairman cried in ecstatic greeting.

The Commissar ignored the greeting. He said,'I must concede you are right about your not being alone. Indeed the Red Tartar Republic is with everybody, and shall refuse to negotiate withdrawals. But where are your passports?'

The Chairman quoted from a one-kepko* tract he had memorized,'The Revolution knows no frontiers!'

'Tramp! Do you presume to educate us on the Law of the World Proletariat?'

'Comrade-sir!' The Chairman-was aghast.

'Now, speak up! What were you planning to do with Tartar tits?

The Chairman answered prayerfully, 'Suck them.'

This prompted a fresh assault; the Committee watched in adoration and awe as each blow landed on the Chairman, studied each swing and delivery, and made elaborate notes to be processed and debated later. The Commissar spoke into a loudspeaker, 'Fall in, Comrades! Tartar tits are in peril!' Soon a crowd of factory hands gathered; the Chairman, having regained consciousness by now, was heartened by the sight of so many class brethren, and he greeted them with the chant that was still popular in Dharmapuri, *Workers of all countries, unite!* The Commissar silenced him, then conferred with his workers, who agreed that the brown vermin had come to lay hands on the Revolution's white bread and pork chops. A team of Confederate espionage agents, visiting the Tartar Republic on a programme of exchange, agreed too, adding,'A threat to White tits anywhere is a threat to world peace.'

Such was the convergence of these two world powers, that the Tartars felt it legitimate to belabour the pilgrims, who now turned and fled, shouting ritual slogans for proletarian solidarity even as they fled, a chant which their Tartar pursuers lustily joined in. The Committee carried home the notes they had taken on the beating, which they hoped would supplement

* The smallest coin in Tartar currency.

their arcana. Few of them, however, reached home. The majority lost their way in their headlong retreat, and wandering through dense forests, were set upon by wild beasts and pernicious insects.

Meanwhile the Tartar courier reached Dharmapuri. The prison doors were opened for him, and he delivered the Great Red Father's edict to the incarcerated Comrades. *Comrades-vermin,* read the crisp command, *partake of the Sacrament!* The Comrades read and re-read the message, they marvelled at how profoundly it expressed the genius of history; the prison wardens saw the baptismal light shine on their faces; this was how they came out of prison, and, in penitence, sought the dung crypts of the Palace. A new era of Eucharistic togetherness had begun between the Communards and the Presidency.

CHAPTER X

A Cameo of Anti-imperialism

When the Communards entered the Hall of the Celestial Birds, as the Parliament of Dharmapuri was known, they did so with the Palace's approval, as did the assorted dissenters who made up the loyal Opposition. In the trauma and ridicule of their lost insurrection, they declined to take the chairs given to them, but crouched instead at the feet of the Partisans of the Holy Spirit. It was widely believed that the Tartar Communards had told them to do so, for reasons of history, occult reasons which the lay world but dimly perceived. From this position of vantage, the Communards kept ceaseless vigil over the Partisans' anti-imperialism, and though the crouch induced sleep, they awoke in fits and starts to scratch their ears and make radical interventions.

It was thus that they awoke during the famous cadaver debate: the debate came about because a Partisan inadvertently questioned the Presidency on a *'Wild West Times'* story which suggested a deal between Confederate professors of anatomy and the generals fighting the Confederacy's war in the Yellow Peninsula. 'We have become too rich,' said the report, 'and our undertakers' lobby too powerful. This makes it difficult to buy cadavers for anatomy lessons. The war ensured a steady supply of coloured corpses. The end of the war might have meant disaster for the medical schools, but for Dharmapuri coming to our rescue with a generous offer...'

'The Venerable Presidency,' the Minister for Trade said, answering the Partisan, 'is not aware of any such compact.'

'We certainly accept that position,' the Partisan said. 'But the capitalist media is insinuating a-barter of corpses for candy.'

'No,' the Minister said.

'Is the Confederacy a belligerent or friend?'

The Minister refused to answer.

'Who owns the *Wild West Times?* The Confederate Intelligence Agency?' the Partisan asked.

The Communard member, crouching at the feet of the Partisan, scratched his ears and woke up, 'Whoever doubts it?'

The Minister, 'We have no information.'

The Partisan, 'Is there a department of cadavers?'

The Minister, 'No.'

The Partisan, 'Are our citizens left unburied when they die?'

The Minister, 'The information is classified.'

The Partisan, 'If they are not buried, where do they go when they die?'

Another Partisan, intervening, 'They transmigrate, of course.'

A Member from the Opposition, 'Do the imperialists transmigrate?'

The Minister, 'We do not wish to comment on the internal affairs of other countries.'

The Communard, from his crouch, made his historic intervention, 'Is the Venerable Presidency aware that the Great Red Tartar Republic, natural ally of all decolonized peoples, has outlawed the transmigration of souls?'

Laughter rocked the House; desiring no part in the merriment, the Communard crouched back to sleep, comforted by the knowledge that the cause had been served for the day.

*

Laavannya sat on the riverside moss and pined for Vaatasena; Siddhaartha consoled her, saying, 'Prison doors will open for him, and he will seek out the Great Mendicant. It is so destined.'

She grew quiet, and said after a while, 'Siddhaartha ...'

'What other sorrow afflicts you, Laavannya?'

She drew Sunanda closer, and said, 'O Siddhaartha, I fear for my child.'

'He is well.'

'The pallor has returned to his face.' She paused awhile, then said, 'Shall we take him to the House of Healing?'

'Must you, Laavannya?'

In the dense canopies of the riverside trees the birds of the night crooned and changed perches; Laavannya said, 'You gave me faith in the trees and the river, yet the mind's old tutored infirmities return, and I think again and again of the House of Healing. Bear with me, Siddhaartha.'

'As you wish,' Siddhaartha said.

At dawn they began their walk back to the city, to the House of Healing.

A crowd milled round the House, sick people and their chaperons, and touts and peddlers of hospital privileges. Over the main archway were inscribed legends celebrating *Shaakuntala*. Siddhaartha read them, and said ruefully, 'Look how we have broken faith with *Shaakuntala* and its forest birds. Little do the apothecaries know that every bird noise is medicament, and that in these gentle sounds and changing colours are stored the cures for all our afflictions.'

As they walked in through the archway, they were stopped by a guard in braid, who, after a brief exchange of pleasantries, came straight to the point, 'What is it going to be? Money or the woman?'

Then he looked at Laavannya intently, his looks searing through her clothes, until she winced and swore; the sick ones and their chaperons, on hearing her swear, broke into giggles. *The hapless woman has lost her senses,* they said, *she does not know the Law. Could she be one of the saboteurs? The Imperialists choose pretty women for spying. Look how the world is envious of Dharmapuri!* Siddhaartha listened to the chatter, and was aware of its perilous drift. Hastily he spoke to the crowd, 'Citizens, this woman here is a kitchen maid come to get her son ministered unto.'

It turned out that the wayfaring King had been indiscreet, because his words set off an exchange which soon grew belligerent. The crowd surrounded him, barring his way on all sides, and called out to its leader, 'O Kumbhaanda! come hither and question the strangers.'

From the corridors emerged a troll-like man of extreme ugliness: Kumbhaanda, the leader. 'Woman,' he asked, 'have you no links with the forces of Imperialism?'

'None,' Siddhaartha said, answering for Laavannya.

Kumbhaanda ignored the reply, and went on with the questioning. 'A week ago the Confederate fleet was in our ocean, pretending to fish. Can you prove they really were fishing?'

'We were not aware of anything,' Siddhaartha said.

'But what evidence,' Kumbhaanda asked, 'do you have that this woman has no links with that fleet?'

'She has no links whatsoever,' Siddhaartha said. 'To that I swear.'

Kumbhaanda's stare blazed with the militancy of the people, and as it moved over her body, Laavannya sensed the imminence of another patriotic encounter.

'Of what use is swearing?' Kumbhaanda scoffed, 'the perjury of lackeys? Instead let us have proof of innocence.'

The crowd approved, and Kumbhaanda drew closer. 'Take off your clothes, woman, and prove your innocence.'

The crowd picked up the command and made a chant of it. Siddhaartha saw a boy, barely out of his teens, chanting louder than the rest; greatly saddened, he walked up to the boy, and laying a tender hand on him, said, 'Child, do you insist that this woman strip?' This provoked more slogans from the crowd of sick men and women. Beneath the frenzy of the slogans a space of quiet opened out for Siddhaartha, in which he ratiocinated futilely: *Even as a prince I had foreseen the doom of Imperialism. Does a woman have to disrobe before a crowd to prove its inevitability?* Siddhaartha sought the boy out once more, and pleaded, 'My child...'

Wetting his girl's-lips with delicate tongue the boy turned on Siddhaartha, 'I have no time for those who whine. I am a Young Partisan and an Anti-imperialist. In this struggle it matters little if this woman is old enough to be my mother.'

Now the slogans grew tumultuous: *Our ocean shall be a zone of peace! The struggle of the Yellow Peninsular people is our struggle! The struggle against the Slovak Spring is our struggle! Strip and reveal the truth!* The cry filled the corridors, *Strip! Strip!* and from the avenue outside, passers-by joined in the chant. Then, suddenly, a sick man in a frenzy broke loose from the crowd and lunged towards Siddhaartha. 'He is the one!' the sick man cried. 'He helps her smuggle in the spies!'

The crowd responded, 'Yes, it is him!'

Soon a new slogan, more frenetic and demanding, rose over the din: *Kill him! Kill, kill!*

Laavannya raised a hand to quieten the crowd; she stood before it, proud mistress of her own body. 'Vile people!' she said.'Here, I will now reveal the Truth you have been hungering for. Look!' Spinning round like a dancer, she cast away her clothes and stood naked before them. 'Do not harm the King!' she said.

Kumbhaanda spoke, 'Yes, we shall spare him, on one condition. The people assembled here, despite their varying ailments of mind and body, and despite the therapy they will soon be undergoing, firmly believe in the ideology of the Celestial Birds. They demand justice. You have called them *vile people,* which is an affront to all those ranged against Imperialism. Therefore, in our considered opinion, mere stripping is not enough. Justice demands a heavier penalty...'

In a world riddled with Imperialist conspiracy the ways of the New Emergent Peoples were complex and of this Laavannya had fair knowledge; yet she failed to anticipate Kumbhaanda's next move. After delivering his pithy speech, he suddenly threw his arms round her waist, and kneeling before her, sought to slake his strange thirst between her legs; the crowd participated with gasps and cheering. The boy with girl's-lips leaned against a wall and looked on. His eyes hungering and unshut, he moved through stimulant gyrations to a solitary orgasm.

Siddhaartha felt a small tug on the hem of his robe; it was

Sunanda.'Ah, my child!' sorrowed Siddhaartha. The boy wept silently, with the quiet of one who has seen countless births and passings. He took the King's arm and led him away. Around them the hot crowd seethed and foamed; Siddhaartha shut his eyes with his palms. He was blotting out the sight of aggregation and violence, the relentless repetition of which has made the history of man. *God!* thought Siddhaartha, *only the blind could look upon it!*

Beneath the palms pressed against his eyes the darkness grew, until it was a dark sea; he sank into its mystic depths and fled along its bed. Far above him, like a caustic spume, sullenly the roar of the crowd exploded.

CHAPTER XI

The Getaway

The crowd had dwindled into a few retreating stragglers when Siddhaartha finally opened his eyes. Laavannya stood amid the litter of her clothes.

'Laavannya' Siddhaartha called. She turned towards him like a sunflower unfolding.

'Siddhaartha, I have sinned in your sight.'

The King gently stopped her mouth with his hand, but her lips moved beneath his fingers, articulating the words that sought forgiveness. Siddhaartha collected her scattered clothing and dressed her. Then he led her and Sunanda through the doorway of the House of Healing. They were now in a dismal length of tunnel along which, over rails sunk in the ground, moved an interminable succession of trolleys. In the trolleys lay the sick, who neither stirred nor groaned. Colliding against Siddhaartha, one of the trolleys came off the rails.

'Disrupter!' the trolley attendant shouted. 'How did you get in here?'

'Pardon us,' Siddhaartha said.

The trolley came to a halt against Siddhaartha, who held on to it to save himself from falling; as he did so, his hand fell on the trolley's occupant. In the trolley lay a woman, cold to the touch.

'God!' Siddhaartha said. 'Is she...?'

'Dead,' the attendant said. 'Yes, she is. Does that perturb you? You ought to be perturbed over the disruption of traffic you have caused.'

'We never meant to,' Siddhaartha said.

'Saboteurs!' the attendant said, raising his voice again. 'Spies!'

Over his cries the endless rumbling of the trolleys continued;

they saw that each trolley carried a preserved cadaver.

'Siddhaartha,' Laavannya said, 'get us out of here.'

Siddhaartha turned back towards the doorway.

'You may not go back that way,' the attendant said.

'We have no desire to hinder your traffic,' Siddhaartha said.

'This corridor is one way, and since you have chosen it, there is no getting away now. Go along with the trolleys, and take care not to derail any more.'

'I see no reason in this.'

'It is the Law,' the attendant said, and losing further interest in their presence, turned to the body of the woman in the trolley and addressed it, 'Maiden! We did not plan this break of journey. But since it has happened, let us make the most of it.'

Saying this he peeled away the shroud; in the feeble light of the tunnel Laavannya saw the body of a woman of stunning beauty, which the scientists of the mortuary had preserved in a state of utmost freshness.

'A scholar from the University of Nalanda,' the attendant said, 'the harem of reactionary learning.' Taking off his own clothes, he mounted the inert body. 'Merchant's daughter! Exploiter of the toiling people! This is class struggle, the Retribution!'

'O Siddhaartha,' Laavannya cried, 'take us away!'

Recovering himself, Siddhaartha steered Laavannya and Sunanda away from the gruesome transgression. As they walked down the corridor, they came upon another man copulating with a corpse on a trolley, and another and yet another. The menacing dusk of the tunnel grew dense with funereal lust.

'I see light,' Siddhaartha said. 'The end of the tunnel.'

Laavannya tugged at his arm. 'Listen, Siddhaartha!'

'I hear it. It is people, crying for their dear ones.'

They walked towards the noise, while the trolleys turned a bend and disappeared into a cavernous chamber. Beyond the corridor was a patio; Siddhaartha was never to forget what he saw there or what he heard; a tableau of men and women and children drawn in the calisthenics of despair, and the ululation of primordial sorrow. The King and his wards waded helplessly through this great sorrowing and reached another entrance over which a signboard read 'Therapy'. Again, a guardsman in braid: 'I shall come straight to the proposition.' The guardsman was affable and talkative. 'What would you like to offer: money or the woman? There is, of course, the boy, and we who man this place, including the physicians, are not averse to pederasty, but the boy is still too young. As you must have realized, this is a one-way journey, and if you go on, you cannot escape the therapy. Did you not see the trolleys?'

'What about the trolleys?' Siddhaartha asked.

'None of them escaped the therapy, that is what. They were all treated at the first therapy centre; this second centre is for those who have missed the first, but of course no law is without its escape chute.'

'It passes my understanding.'

'I guessed as much. An alien, are you?'

'Yes, sir.'

'From which country are you, alien?'

'Oh, mine is a lost kingdom.'

'Very well. What is your trade?'

'King,' Siddhaartha said, with guilt and hesitation.

'Ah, there are trades and trades,' the guardsman said. 'I might as well confide in you, King. Each cadaver shipped out to the Confederacy brings money to the exchequer, and much of this money goes into our campaigns against Imperialism. You cannot possibly guess, being a mere King, how much an anti-imperialist diplomatic event costs. I have the figures here, if you care to read...'

'Some other time,' Siddhaartha said.

'As you wish. But remember, this is monetary science. Our medical schools sell diplomas and the money goes into the campaign. Do you get me?'

'I do.'

'Our doctors learn enough to turn out cadavers, so there is money saved abroad for Ministers and Partisans who go to the

Confederacy for treatment. And when they convalesce out there, they take the campaign right into the citadel of Imperialism. This brilliant harnessing of gains for eventual use in the struggle of the people we call Surplus Value.'

'I am enlightened.'

'Look how the Celestial Birds triumph over Imperialism! If we keep back the corpses, there will be no instruction in the Confederate schools of medicine, and the Confederates will go without ministration.'

'But, sir,' Siddhaartha said, 'I thought you told me it was your leaders who went to the Confederacy for cures.'

The guardsman was visibly annoyed. 'You speak unwisely! You forget the Great Crisis. Under the Crisis Laws you can be killed and shipped straightaway, without the formality of therapy, but that is far from my intention. I am a peaceable man and a connoisseur and see that your woman is of exquisite breed. If you let me and the four physicians inside have her, we will ship only the boy. If however you add a thousand silvers to the bargain, all three of you can slip away to freedom through this trap door.'

Sunanda started wailing loudly, and clung to Laavannya and Siddhaartha.

'I repeat,' the guardsman said, 'it is a bargain. I offer it to you because I am rather fond of you. Remember, a clean Dharma corpse fetches twenty thousand silvers worth of hard currency in the Confederacy. My kickback at a thousand silvers a corpse is three thousand silvers, and yet I promise to let you go.'

Siddhaartha did not reply; in his forehead opened an invisible eye, a confluence of energies, compassionate; its gaze stilled the guardsman who slumped to the floor. The veil of unknowing fell away from the fallen minion; he looked up in the gratitude of baptism, in the peace that had come over his festering elements. Said the guardsman, *My Prince, you have found me at last!* Said Siddhaartha, *I still seek,* and his love surged for the sinning and the decrepit. From inside the chamber of therapy peeped out physicians and guardsmen;

Siddhaartha touched them, and their elements too came apart, and their breath sought the subtle apertures for flight. Presently they all lay still for-ever.

'Come, my children,' said Siddhaartha, taking Laavannya and Sunanda by the hand. He led them through the patio. In the grey outer wall of stone a casement opened for Siddhaartha. Like the roots of a plant which seek their way through the dark damp trust of the earth, the King, the kitchen maid and the child began their journey.

CHAPTER XII

The Man Who Sorrowed

Both the Red Tartar Republic and the White Confederacy depended a great deal on their allies, and so these global principals often tested the stability of their hirelings. These tests were mostly performed on the allies' concubines, who therefore assumed much geo-political consequence. Samarkhand, a decolonized principality bordering Dharmapuri, was a client of Imperialism. When a Confederate trading house in Samarkhand sent out of its employ the husband of the Prime Minister's most favoured concubine, it was evident to Samarkhand that its political stability was being probed. In swift and brilliant retaliation, the Prime Minister withheld the supply of fresh eggs to Confederate submarines docked in its ports. When the submariners decided to breakfast without eggs, Samarkhand began contemplating other means of vindication.

*

The concubine sat on the Prime Minister's bed, disconsolate; Samarkhand's ruler reclined on cushions of down and watched her distress indulgently.

'O fair cow-elephant!' he said. 'Imperialism will soon discover they have a doughtier ally in me than they had bargained for, one who has the entire population behind him. To prove this we will presently conclude a treaty of war with our great neighbour, Dharmapuri.'

'A treaty, sire?' the concubine asked. 'Of war?'

'Lie down beside me, and let me instruct you in the mysteries of state.'

She lay down as commanded, an eager novice, while he began playing on her skin with his fingers as on the stretched hide of a drum.

'Compute, O harlot,' he said, 'as an initial exercise, the cost of time of the earth's rulers. A million gold for every minute of my reign. How many of them do I drum away on you?'

'I have not kept count of the minutes, sire. But it is no small joy to know that this humble one too is part of the gold standard.'

'Compute then the cost of my entire reign. Samarkhand will never be able to pay it back. Yet,' he paused, 'fantasies of your infidelity assail me.'

'Beloved Lord,' the concubine said, 'you pain me speaking thus.'

'Causing you pain is indeed far from my mind. The truth is, I know you greatly resent the proximity of your husband, those chance intimacies. And therefore I had contemplated snuffing him out, and almost ordered my Officers of Justice ...'

'.... to stage a highway accident?' the concubine completed.

'You are learning fast!'

'O citizen-monarch, but I am becoming confused as well. I have heard it said that Dharmapuri, ruled as it is by pharisaic dissemblers, practised these cruelties, but Samarkhand with its great past and God-given laws ....'

'I am pleased that you realize our laws are God-given and administered to justify God's ways. Now, coming back to your husband, on second thoughts, I decided against liquidation, because, were your husband to be removed, you would become mine and mine alone. Where then, O delectable whore, would be the pleasure of prevailing over the adversary? Divested of such triumph, of what use would be my power and sovereignty?'

The pedagogy of state tired the concubine; *I do not want to know,* she said to herself, and fell back on the one familiar certitude of nationhood, this bed of her thwarted orgasms. She lay there in dutiful pretence and opened her flower for her sovereign. The Prime Minister went on, 'Clausewitz has said that war is the pursuit of politics by other means, but he never understood that wars could be agreed on for common purposes. Our problems and Dharmapuri's are similar, and their President has been enquiring recently if we, for the common good, could have another war of togetherness. The treaty will be for such a war.'

'Which will leave a few thousand soldiers dead?' A militant sorrow welled in her, the bond between concubine and foot soldier, the solidarity of the hired and the exploited; she sorrowed for a thousand boys slain by the treaty, a thousand lovers slain in their prime; desiring them, she rose in anger letting the sovereign's manhood slip out of her.

'Sire,' she said, 'we have had seven wars with Dharmapuri. Were all of them wars of togetherness?'

'They were, truly.'

'God!'

'The science of state ...' pleaded the Prime Minister.

The concubine grew even more unhappy. 'I fail to grasp the intricacies of that science, sire, hindered as I am with this high intelligence of mine. They had diagnosed my intelligence at school; the matron, a kindly woman, got me funds for corrective surgery. "Moon-face", she said, "surgery would make you a handsome cretin, a prospective leader of our people." But my mother wailed and wept before the surgeons, who let me off with the warning not to show up at school, or before the Thought Police. Thus I learned no trade save the one I could pursue with my body.'

The Prime Minister regarded her fondly. 'Surely, you have not regretted it?'

'Far from it, sire,' the concubine said, feeling the bed of down with her hands. 'Have I not reached places where few women have reached, and beyond which there is no reaching?'

'And yet,' said the Prime Minister, 'you have ejected my manhood.'

'Ah, miserable me,' the concubine said, 'causing you distress over a mere fantasy of war! Forgive me, my Lord, and grace me by entering me again.'

The Prime Minister did so, simultaneously pursuing the pedagogy of state, 'If we launch this war, the ensuing tide of patriotism in both the countries will greatly strengthen the respective regimes. Thus will the trading houses be intimidated.'

'And what happens if we lose?'

'Innocent one! In Samarkhand I win, and in Dharmapuri, its President.'

'Oh, those dead — they lose!'

Again her anger rose for the bodies, for lovers thrown away in grotesque offering; it caused a distemper to pass from the damp between her thighs to the Prime Minister's organ. 'Forgive me, sire,' the concubine said, giving up.

The Prime Minister sought an orgasm in anxious haste. 'Our time is running out; he said. 'In an hour my Begum returns.'

'And where, sire, has Her Excellency gone?'

The Prime Minister began a rambling reply, 'Samarkhand needs to replenish its wardrobes and cellars; ships are on their way with bales of silk and kegs of wine, and we have no money to pay for the cargo.'

'But where is the Begum?' the concubine persisted.

The Prime Minister grew dispirited. 'Today she goes to bed with a Confederate credit agency.'

'A whole agency, sire?'

'Yes, a whole agency.'

The vision of her nation as a pimp, its armed legions and its flying machines and flotillas, its spies and prosecutors and judges, its convocations, protocols and glittering ceremony, all the many arms of a pimp-god, made the concubine sad. She sensed in her decrepit lover a greater sadness, and knew that it was her turn now to use the pedagogy of state to resurrect him; so she spoke to him of Samarkhand's history and mission, of the eventual overcoming, and of the great orgasms of glory. But he stopped her saying, 'Whore! All I want is my erection!' He was peeved with himself and with Samarkhand, with its war and history; the tragedy of state unfolded itself before the concubine in the emptiness of its exchequer and the impotence of its Prime Minister. In great pity and giving, like the kitchen maid of Dharmapuri, she bent over him, and taking his limp worm in her hands sought to heal him not with heroic legend but with the glances of the eternal temptress. Yet behind those glances lay her tears, in turgid subterranean pools. She spoke, 'Look at my lips, my lover-Lord, the lips my husband kissed on our nuptial night. Have you not seized these lips, and in this capture won your war? Rejoice, for with these lips shall I rouse you presently.' She clapped her hands, and from behind the curtains and over the transmission net work, swelled the anthem of Samarkhand.

*

In a tavern in Shantigrama a group of citizens sat round a luminary from the Press to hear about the new Sorrow with Samarkhand. Karikaala, the communicator, said, 'I have secret sources, all of them infallible.'

Sensing the scepticism of his listeners, he pulled out of his satchel a bundle of rags from which arose a dizzying stench.

'You cannot guess,' Karikaala said, 'what lies hidden inside these rags.'

'A dead rat?' suggested an irreverent citizen.

'Treason!' Karikaala said. 'What I hold hidden here,' the communicator paused and looked round, '... is the menstrual pad of no less a person than the Media Minister Simhamukha's wife. This is from her last menstruation; my exclusive scoop and my proof of veracity.'

There was stunned disbelief, then abject acceptance; the citizens passed the bundle round, taking turns to sniff the pad in veneration. They now knew that Karikaala could be believed, for could he not reach out to the bleeding springs of the most beautiful and powerful women of Dharmapuri?

'You are patriots,' Karikaala said, 'and I will take you into confidence. There is a new Imperialist conspiracy against Dharmapuri, but we will launch a Sorrow against Samarkhand to pre empt it. Our Persuaders will deal with the external adversary, but we need more secret policemen to defeat the enemy within.'

The citizens agreed that this was necessary; the scribe continued, 'To keep the secret policemen occupied, we need more enemies.'

In awe of that reasoning the listeners assented, and Karikaala said, 'Tomorrow, at dawn, our Persuaders cross the boundary, and so too the soldiers of Samarkhand. There will then be shooting and occupation, and of course rape, which will be filmed for analysis by our leaders.'

'Can we see it too?' the citizens asked. 'Just the rape?'

'Patience,' Karikaala said. 'I promise that everyone of you, God willing, will get a chance.'

Karikaala's and the citizens' phalluses distended in anticipation; then, suddenly, darkness fell on the tavern, and the risen organs, swaying like serpents, gazed into the unnatural night with cyclops' eyes. In the dark they heard the voice of a little girl, 'Spare me the pain, I cannot endure it again.'

Karikaala sprang up in terror, crying, 'Stop it! Who are you?'

The voice answered, 'I am Kaanchanamaala.'

'Who?' Karikaala demanded.

'Kanakalata's blind daughter,' the voice said.

'Go away!' Karikaala said. 'No one needs you here!'

'Yes, gentle sirs,' the voice said 'I shall go.'

And it trailed away into the dark.

Ka twam baale? Kaanchanamaala.
Kasya putree? Kanakalataya.
Kim te haste? Taalee patram.
Kaava rekha? Ka Kha Ga Gha.

Over the din of battles rose child voices chanting the doggerel of innocence; the chanting died away and the darkness lifted; the Cyclops' eyes blinked, unquiet. The men sat dazed and still; then one of them rose, possessed, and, smearing his forehead with the slop of the tavern floor in hysterical penitence, started wailing. Karikaala admonished him, 'Get a hold on yourself, citizen! A Sorrow is to break out, and it is the hour of preparedness.'

The man cried and said, 'I do not want to prepare. All I want is to seat my child on my lap.'

His body swayed, and like the rain in the forest his crying rose,'I want my little daughter!'

CHAPTER XIII

The Legion of the Baptised

The Sorrow and its accompanying patriotism filled the news-papers, and the people gluttonously consumed the printed excrescence. The Sorrow was painted on countless canvases, sculpted, rendered into rhyme, danced; women parted with their gold so that the Persuaders could buy more implements of persuasion, and little children took to the streets with evil and violent chants. The Persuaders' wives alone blasphemed. To their angry cantonment returned the first veteran of the Samark-hand Sorrow, limping home on one leg and blind in one eye. He hopped to his wife, and in the pirouetting of the maimed, took her into his feeble embrace. The women of the canton-ment gathered round him, and a Partisan welcomed him home with garlands and flowers.

'Beloved one,' the Persuader said to his woman, 'from this day I set you free.'

The woman concluded that injury had distracted him, but the Persuader, divining her thoughts, spoke thus, 'You presume that a deranged mind accounts for my words. Rest assured my mind is whole, and I speak with a Persuader's responsibility. I want to make you aware of a change in our circumstance: my genitals have been shorn by flying shrapnel, a most intimate sacrifice for the Motherland...'

The woman screamed and fainted. With much ministration they revived her, and the Partisan spoke, although with some embarrassment, 'Heroic wife! How many are fortunate enough to share such sacrifice?'

'Our leader speaks truly,' the maimed Persuader said. 'Woman, look into this satchel of mine: it is full of medals,

73

decorations for heroic Sorrowing.'

From the crowd of blaspheming wives, Mandakini stepped forward, and said, 'Leader, Partisan! Intercede with the Motherland, and pray that she takes back the medals and returns the genitals.'

This stunned the listeners, and the Partisan cried, 'Treason!'

'Be it treason,' Mandakini said.

She faced the Partisan, and parting her garments, dazzled him with her body.

'Partisan, old man,' she said, 'look where you had starved me these fourteen years. I curse you in that hunger!'

She draped herself again; the Partisan, captivated by the sight of her thighs and navel, implored her to keep them bared a little longer, and upon her refusal was greatly incensed.

'Saboteurs of the Resistance!' he swore.

Mandakini ignored him, and pulled out a pair of scissors from her girdle. Offering it to the maimed Persuader, she said, 'Take this, hireling, and snip away this decrepit Partisan's genitals. Let us then hear what he has to say about the Motherland.'

'Treason!' the Persuader cried.

Mandakini held the scissors up, and asked the women gathered there, 'Who among you would like to wield this?'

The Persuaders' wives surged forward, a tide of vengefulness, of grief and compassion, and scores of hands sought to grab the instrument of justice.

*

The news of this encounter swept over Shantigrama, and soon the sordid nights of the Partisans were filled with the gentle and terrifying snip of scissors, charmed weapons worked by lovely fingers; anti-imperialism now turned into castration-neurosis. Secret policemen combed the city for women with scissors and hundreds of bewildered seamstresses were thrown into prison.

*

After remaining in hiding for a while, Mandakini sneaked back into her house. Ghrini accompanied her.

'Where is Aryadatta?' Ghrini asked.

'Still in hiding,' Mandakini said.

'And Sreelata?'

'Here in the bath, my lover,' Sreelata said from inside the house. 'Come in and watch me bathe my beautiful body.'

'Mandakini,' Ghrini said, 'we are being hunted.'

Mandakini listened and smiled. A presence that grew on her, that enfolded her in fond play, was telling her that there was nothing to do any more, nothing more to resist. Presently Sree-lata came out of the bath, the paste of fragrant sandal on her breasts. Mandakini kissed those breasts, and said, 'Sreelata, the conflict has ended.' Sreelata moved on to Ghrini and kissed him and asked, 'Is it ended for you too?'

Then there came knocks on the door.

'Go, Ghrini, see who knocks,' Mandakini said.

'They have come for us,' Ghrini said.

The knocks continued.

'Go,' said Sreelata.

Ghrini tiptoed to the door and opened it.

'You, Sir!' he said, in disbelief.

'Yes, I, your General,' said Paraashara, who stood in the doorway, garlanded with flowers. Paraashara entered the house, and touched the women with his hands.

'The hour of baptism has come,' he said.

'Ah, my General,' asked Mandakini, 'Who was it that baptised you?'

They stood long in contemplation of one another; a laughter arose outside and lashed the far ridges.

'He that baptised me,' Paraashara said, 'flees along the river bank. I shall march at the head of his legion.'

The laughter grew insistent. 'It calls me,' Mandakini said.

'We come,' Sreelata said.

Outside, the grassland and the infinitude of a pathway. The women and the boy-soldier stepped on to the grass, and the

General led them.

*

That night a mammoth procession of patriotic resistance wended its way through Shantigrama. Communards and rope dancers, courtesans and many others from diverse and grotesque persuasions marched behind the Partisans of the Holy Spirit. In the chant of the multitude were lost the individual voices; the chant, like a blind serpent, moved on to blot out the sights and minds of men.

At the head of this carnival, on his precarious crutches, hobbled the castrated Persuader.

CHAPTER XIV

The Slumbering Seeds

The procession swirled through the city; householders gazed upon it and were overwhelmed. They saw in it their own aggregation, a thing they had conjured out of their pride and their servitude. It assailed them with its aggregate footfall and smothered their reason; *it is we,* they thought, *it is Dharmapuri* and were bewildered, and soon the very bewilderment became their refuge. When the footfall had died away, and the trail was quiet once again, other voices fell on their ears: their own slumbering seeds from the future spoke to them. *Inglorious fathers!* said the accusing voices, *you have sought to blight us while we slept through the incubatory ages; like termites you beset the palm-leaves on which is chronicled our coming; we will come cleansed in our penances, and born fatherless, we will cast you into the fires of sacrifice. You built your cities over the roots of the compassionate* pipals, *you laid your burdens of evil on the loves of free men and the beasts of the wild. We will come to avenge these in a tumultuous becoming of leaf and root, in the canopy of the insurgent forest.* Now that the mob had passed, the citizens of Dharmapuri, lonely and afraid, listened to the voices which sought them out in their isolation and unable to bear the wrath of prophecy, they stopped their ears with their palms. When the fear abated, they opened their ears again and petitioned the Partisans. *Leaders, Partisans!* they cried, *reassure us with the Sacrament.* They bared themselves, and cried, *Geld us, Sires, as you do the beasts of the plough, for from within our sperm our seeds cry out, and we cannot bear that cry.* The women bared themselves too, *Partisans, Rulers, Fathers of the Armies and the Wars! Whore in us, sow your dissolute seeds, let*

77

beasts of slaughter be born of us, flocks of docile goats.

*

The cry of the goat echoed through the Palace, and the guardsmen and servitors, stirred by its lust, whispered to one another,'The President takes a new woman!' In his bedchamber, the President lay spent beside the woman he had so honoured with the goat-cry. Waking up from his stupor, he said, 'I am well pleased in her. Whose wife is she?'

'Sire,' answered the Military Secretary, peeping out from behind the curtains, 'She is the wife of. The Venerable Hayavadana.'

'Hayavadana, who?' the President asked.

'The Vice-Minister of Aircraft, Sire.'

'Who?'

To refresh the President's memory, the Keeper of Memories brought forth a dossier from which he read, 'In the Year of the Famine, the Venerable Hayavadana, who worked as a kitchen boy in the Palace, was sent to the Venerable President to fulfil an experience of pederasty...'

'Yes, I remember,' the President said.'He had large breasts.'

The Keeper of Memories was in a quandary; with much bowing and grovelling and ritual salutation of the Sacrament, he said,'Wise and all-seeing Lord! The breasts were on the Venerable Hayavadana's wife.'

Hayavadana's wife coyly felt her breasts, then resumed her posture of adoration.

'It is true,' the President said. 'At times my memory does fail me.'

'My Lord,' the Keeper of Memories said,'the nation cannot grudge you so slight a slip. You who spend every hour of your waking in the service of your dear subjects....'

'Vermin!' the President swore.

'Sire?' quavered the Keeper of Memories, wetting his bark.

'I have no memory loss!'

'Your Grace remembers everything.'

'I remember the kitchen boy with fair thighs and lush lips,' the President said; the Venerable Hayavadana's wife raised her folded hands and uttered praises to the Sacrament. The President turned towards the Keeper of Memories, and forgiving him, said, 'Tell me what followed.'

Maids with mops cleaned away the slop from around the feet of the Keeper of Memories, even as he squirmed inside his wet apparel, embarrassed and cold. He read on from the dossier:'The Venerable Hayavadana had been spending his days quietly as the beloved of the Palace cook; but upon the success of the aforesaid experiment in pederasty, the Venerable President decided to elevate the Venerable Hayavadana to the Vice-Ministership of Aircraft.' The President looked at the woman; his feeble discharge between her legs clotted obscenely.

'Go,' said the President, irritated by the clot,'clean yourself and come back to me.'

She rose, bent low, and withdrew into the toilet chamber; there she sobbed and retched, taking care to vomit as quietly as she could. She heard the goat-cry summoning her to bed again. When she presented herself, the President asked, 'Woman, what is your name?'

'Priyamvada, sire.' she said.

'Now I remember it all,' the President said. 'Your husband's lips were more lush than yours.'

'So they are, sire,' Priyamvada said.

'I am pleased,' the President said.'What favour would you ask of me?'

'Your love, sire, and your mercy.'

'The memory of your husband,' the President said, 'causes me great pleasure.'

In that memory the President ejaculated, and sat back in a state of stupefaction and generosity; and Priyamvada, emboldened, said 'My Lord! My husband of the lush lips is a mere Vice-Minister in an obscure portfolio. May it please your grace to make him the Minister for Sorrowing.'

'Be that done,' the President said; having delivered this fiat he lay back and stretched and soon was fast asleep. The paramount ruler of Dharmapuri lay naked, a snore churning his mouth's odorous fester, and his organ of pleasure fallen limp. Around this the Persuaders gathered in an awesome formation. They guarded the Palace and the city, and the dreary length of the country's frontiers; they guarded at the heart of this impenetrable encirclement, in its dark and central privacy, a malodorous mouth and an incomplete orgasm.

Priyamvada left the sleeping President, and walked, imperiously naked, into the chamber of the President's Principal Secretary. Her nakedness greatly unsettled the officer; Priyamvada stared intently at his visible arousal. 'Your arousal is an affront to the Presidency. It is treason.'

'Spare this wretch, O Gracious One,' the officer said.

'I shall, on condition that you comply with my wishes.'

'I await Your Grace's pleasure.'

'My husband, Hayavadana of the lush lips, has been elevated as the Minister for Sorrowing,' Priyamvada said. 'The Venerable President has willed it. Prepare the Presidential order.'

The Secretary protested weakly, 'I have not received the Presidential palm-leaf,' at which Priyamvada swore, and the Secretary, in a paroxysm of fear, sullied his clothes. Then he rose from his chair and knelt.

'Dog!' said Priyamvada. 'Write!'

Newspapers the next day put forth the story of the reconstitution, and carried elaborate and learned commentaries on the event. Rumannuaan, among all the Ministers, was the staunchest friend of the Tartar Republic but *Prava* wrote, 'The changes undoubtedly bespeak a firmer commitment to anti-imperialism. The new Minister for Dharmapuri's armed forces will keep the adjoining waters a zone of peace, and endeavour to demolish the Imperialist ocean bases.' The Communards of Dharmapuri, hitherto Rumannuaan's die-hard supporters, spoke of him no more; instead they traced Dharmapuri's traditions of anti-imperialism to Hayavadana of the lush lips.

Rumannuaan sat at the Palace Gate, and smearing his locks with the dust and slop of the road, set up a low, piercing dirge. The President heard it, and ordered him into his presence. The old man made his way in, crawling and grovelling.

'Mercy,' he said 'Lord, have mercy!'

The merciful President made Rumannuaan a Minister Without Portfolio, and gave him the use of his mansion and his kitchen-maids. In gratitude Rumannuaan held out his hands and begged,

'Sacrament, My Lord!'

*

Rumannuaan walked back to his mansion, chewing the dung, in the joy of restoration... Siddhaartha, in flight along the river-bank, past the green fortresses of trees, said, 'Laavannya, I sense a great tremor.' Laavannya stood still. The wind blew against the current of the river. Siddhaartha said,'Listen, Laavannya!'

'Cause me to hear it, Siddhaartha.'

Siddhaartha laid his hand on her forehead.'In times far away, in times yet to be, the seeds of man and plant stir in anger. In those times I see man reborn a resplendent animal, I see the plant overcoming the edifices of the city.'

Laavannya listened. The wind died down in the clouds and on the mountain. Now it swept within the layered earth. Beneath the earth, in the fires of the earth, the *pipal* seeds, and beyond the countless renewals of the womb, the seeds of man, cried out their coming.

CHAPTER XV

The Celestial Birds

It was the anger of the unborn that raged as wind and fire within the earth; the waifs of the city walked the streets too weary for anger. The dusk froze, and Shantigrama's glittering facades lit up. One of the wandering children said to himself, *I am hungry;* he was a child of eight, and in his hands he carried a bundle of newspapers he was to sell that evening. No one seemed to want to buy. Everyone walked past him, and because he felt intimidated, he could not stop them; they were beautiful men and women, the evening was filled with the carnival noises of their pleasure and waste. He held out his bundle with a desultory hawker's cry, which he lowered in order not to annoy the beautiful people. Soon the cry was a private chant to himself.

He was cold. He laid his burden on the steps before a shop, and trusting all mankind not to steal it, wandered off to look in at the shop windows. He pressed his face against a pane behind which rows of rabbits and elephants and elves nodded their heads. For a little while they were all his, in the possessing magic of his child's desire; then he tired of them and moved on to another window where he saw piles of confectionery. His hunger too was an enchantment, but then it was pain; his feet faltered and he became sad. He came back and sat on the steps where he had left his newspapers, and gathering himself up like a little bird, fell asleep. And sitting asleep by the roadside, the little boy dreamed. In his dream he had returned home without selling any of his newspapers. He saw the inside of his hut: his mother squatting on the floor and his little brothers and sisters in a crowd of twins and triplets clinging to her tits, noisy in their hunger. His step-father, father of his brothers and sisters, was trying to beat his children off and get hold of his wife's breasts.

The children cried in pain, but his mother neither spoke nor moved.

Her husband grew very angry. 'Why don't you send them away, abandon them in the forest?'

At that moment a Partisan appeared inside the hut.

'Look at this brood,' the Partisan said. 'You mate and breed without restraint, and then call upon us to herd them and rule over them.'

'What you say is the truth, sir,' the boy's step-father said. And saying so, he peeled away his woman's clothes. Still she neither spoke nor moved.

'What are you doing to the woman?' the Partisan asked.

'Hunger!' the woman's husband said. 'I must quench my hunger with my woman's milk.

Like little animals who have had their prey taken from them, the children clamoured even more. Looking at them uncomfortably, the Partisan spoke to their father. 'You have fallen into this poverty, because you have begotten so many of them. Perhaps you are not aware of the advice given us by the agencies of international credit to induce famines if we fail to control birth by other means. Now, stop that! why are you stroking her breasts so much? It arouses me.'

'Go on with your discourse, sir. I am listening. I stroke her breasts so that the milk wells in them.'

'I shall go on. But if I see too much of that breast being stroked, I might ejaculate.'

'Sir, let your mind not dwell on the breast, but on the programme of reconstruction, on which we have all pinned our hopes.'

'Not by breast alone, but by every other member of her body am I tormented.'

'I entreat you, sir, to go on with the discourse on international banking and our revolution. I am always greatly aroused by ideology.'

'You do love your country, citizen. Some day, I wish you become a Partisan yourself.'

'I too desire it, sir. But till then I need to quieten my hungering guts, and therefore keep stroking her breasts so the milk fills
them. And that is why, much against national policy, I give her
no respite from pregnancy. Because I cannot milk her unless
she whelps. Moreover, what toy save her genitals has this
woman, or for that matter anyone in the black and brown
continents?'

Having said this, he laughed raucously. The woman's breasts,
aroused, were full of milk now. Once again, he beat his children
off, and appeased his hunger with noisy slurps.

'How is the milk?' the Partisan asked.

'You will not be disappointed,' the man said.'Pushpamukhee,
my wife! Let our venerable Partisan have a mouthful of your
milk. This is when we ought to be behind him, because the
enemy wars against us.'

The boy who stood unseen at the door saw and heard all this.
He saw the old Partisan kneel beside his mother and take her tit
between slavering lips. The Partisan stripped himself and put
his clothes aside.

'That is great sagacity, sir,' the woman's husband said. 'There
is always the risk of clothes being sullied by an unguarded
discharge.'

'You have spoken well. But let me tell you this: the Presidency is seeking ways to trade our breast milk for hard currency.'

'Five silvers,' the woman's husband told the Partisan, 'for the
breast milk here.'

The old man counted out the coins, fell to, and very quickly
had his whimper of a climax and rolled over onto his back.

'Pushpamukhee, my beloved!' her husband said to the woman.'Sing the Anthem, for our venerable Partisan has discharged.'

She neither sang nor stirred, while at the door the boy stood
and gazed on. His eyes grew into stars and shone with a light
cold as dew. He wondered why his mother and brothers and
sisters could not see him, then remembered it was a dream.
There was nothing a 'child could not do in a dream. He could
become a bird, a snake, he could turn invisible as he had done.

'Pushpamukhee,' her husband said in rage, 'you have ignored my enjoinment and failed to wake the Partisan with the Anthem. I will not tolerate insolence. If ever you let your tits run dry, I will denounce you to the secret police. Let the Partisan sleep now, while I see if there is any more milk left in your breasts.'

He stroked her breasts and sucked them, and they yielded one last ooze. The children's cry was now an incessant dirge. As the pap went dry, her husband took his lips away, and said, 'Woman, I know you are disregarding me. But I know too that you lust for my nursing. Each time you are with child you cannot wait for me to get to your breasts, and elsewhere. Here, I take these five silvers and go to the tavern for a draught of sour brew and a meal of pig's gut.'

At last the woman spoke. 'You have sucked dry the pus of my breasts, and now you rob my children of these five silvers. Oh, what do I feed them with?'

Her husband brought up a gob of phlegm and spat it on her tits; she did not raise her hand to wipe it off; the phlegm mingled with the residual ooze. She sat impassive.

'My little ones,' she said, 'ungrown and misshapen, will fetch no price even if they are shipped as cadavers.'

'That is because the State is incompetent,' her husband said.

'Why do we have to sell cadavers to Confederate medical schools?

Why don't we take the soft hides of children and make wallets and lamp shades and objects of art? Did not a great leader teach the Aryans to utilize thus the hides of Semite children? We too need such a leader...'

'God willing,' the Partisan said, waking as if on cue, 'we too will have such a leader!'

At this the woman rose. She gathered together her children to herself, and lamented aloud,'I will not let my children be made into wallets!'

'Quiet, woman!' the Partisan said.'Think of the country ...'

She tossed her tresses about and wailed. From the door the boy watched his mother with the cold stars that were his eyes.

'O Partisan, leader,' said his mother, 'those five silvers have been taken away. Give me another, just one more, so that I may buy my children some food.'

'O Partisan, leader,' said her husband, 'give her nothing! Let her pestilential brood starve. Her eldest, her first man's son, has gone out to sell newspapers. Let him bring in his pieces of copper.'

'That is well spoken. That is the way of self-reliance.' From where he stood unseen, enveloped by enchantment, the boy said, *I sold no newspapers this evening.*

'He sold no newspapers this evening,' said his mother. 'This is a cold evening and night. He sits now on the steps of a shop, just the way he curled inside my womb. He sleeps.'

The boy heard this and laughed.

You are wrong, mother, he said. *I am not sleeping, I am dreaming.*

'If he comes back without his pieces of copper,' his step-father said, 'I will kill him.'

The little children stretched their hands towards their mother's breast again where the gob of their father's spit was congealing. Their father fell on them, and hit them viciously again and again; then he cried, 'God, my God! I have raised my hands against my own children!'

He beat his hands on the floor as he lamented; the palms of his hands became blood-spattered and the severed fingers fell away. The boy laughed again. He turned his dream into a castle. Guardsmen stood behind him, their brocades glittering and their scimitars drawn. The boy now called out in a voice that reached out beyond the dream, *Mother!*

His mother heard him, and turned towards the door.

I am an enchanter, mother, the boy said. *Close your eyes and open them again, and you will see me.*

She did as she was told, and rejoiced to see her son. *How you have grown, my son, and how soon! Oh, my little one, will you save me from this evil man?*

The boy unsheathed a glistening sword, and hewed down his

step-father as one would a plant. His mother was pleased. He put the Partisan also to the sword. His brothers and sisters were little worms now, caterpillars; they scurried and hid, then grew wings and flew away laughing.

Come, mother, said the boy, *let me smear these on your breasts and your thighs, these perfumes of the play girls of the city.*

His mother became young once again, like the women who had walked past him as he clung to his bundle of newspapers; she was beautiful like them, and enveloped in their fragrances.

I will give you a palace to live in, mother, the boy said. *And very evening a jewelled prince for your pleasure. I will make you, mother, the prized courtesan of the city.*

She became a courtesan, she shone, and held him close. He clasped her breasts with young-old hands, took his lips away from the suckling tits and looked around. *Where are we, mother? This is a strange night.*

The night of the dream has ended, she said. *This is the night of death.*

*

The mob milled round the white man who stood in the street with his tele-camera. From their midst walked a Partisan who accosted him.

'Did you expose your films?' the Partisan asked.

'I am a film maker,' the white man said.

'And what have you recorded in your instrument?'

'This street....'

Near his bundle of unsold newspapers, his dream ended, the child lay dead.

'Did you record this?' demanded the Partisan.

'I make documentaries.....'

'Who do you make them for?'

'For television companies back home.'

The mob yelled,'Down with spies of Imperialism!'

'So now the truth comes out,' the Partisan said. 'Evidently, you

87

were left here by the Imperialist fleet. I shall not dwell on it for the present, but speak of the child instead. He is a citizen of Dharmapuri who has cast off his body using the ancient knowledge of our sages. Shortly the birds will come hither to cover him with leaves; even the World Bank is familiar with this.'

Someone snatched away the camera, and the slogans rose to a deafening pitch, when a Tartar television crew arrived on the scene. The Partisan asked them, "And what might *you* be filming?'

'Dharmapuri's peace and progress,' said the Tartars,' its *Shaakuntala.*'

The mob applauded, and the Tartars went on,'And of course, the happy children of Dharmapuri.'

Presently a posse of policemen came and took the Imperialist away. The Partisan stooped ceremonially and picked up the little corpse, light in death. Holding up the dry, crisp cadaver with ease, he cried out to the mob, 'Behold the one martyred by Imperialism!'

The mob's fury was like a blistering sand-storm. Carrying the little corpse, the people marched in procession; the road seemed interminable, turning on itself, an eddy of madness. Over them passed a serene flight of *shakuntaas,* the birds of Shaakuntala. The *shakuntaas* spoke among themselves:

'Let us not touch down. This is a city of sin.'

'Look, down below! The city's cruel sacrifice.'

And as the [5] shakuntaas[5] flew on, a little bird which flew along with them said, 'Do not sorrow, for I am born again as one of you.'

The mob below was blinded by its anger, the city's revellers imprisoned by the perfumes on their bodies; no one saw the flight of the Celestial Birds. The birds flew among the stars, above the dust, their sails showing a dull sheen in the starlight, a jewelled flotilla. They spoke once more among themselves:

'Fly on to the Great Pipal.'

'The King meditates under it.'

'We are the Bodhisattva's witnesses.'

CHAPTER XVI

The Night of the Bondsman

In time's slow cycles of endurance there comes now and again an unexpected pinnacle of imperious power. Such power arose one night in Shantigrama, waking the prisoner, Vaatasena, Laavannya's husband. He got up from his bed, and gripping the bars of his prison door, grieved for his child. The guards' feet, heavily shod with hide and metal, ground dully along the corridors, and the clocks of the night chimed tardily. *Sleep, servitors!* commanded Vaatasena, and the guards fell asleep. In his proud sorrow Vaatasena willed that the bars of the prison give way; they whined and bent, making a magical pathway for the prisoner. The prison slept, bound by the dream of the bondsman, its corridors laced with the breath of wardens frozen over their weapons. Vaatasena walked past them and out of the prison gate. Outside the prison were the prisons of free men, the homes of the city and the paved roads which imprisoned the footfall of the traveller; over it all the full moon kept watch.

In the prisons they carried around themselves slept the burdened ones. The whore and the kitchen maid slept in the knowledge of this night's benediction; but those that ruled over them, the calloused old men, tossed sleepless on beds of silk and down. Drugs did not calm them, nor did their maids rouse them; their lusts simmered unrisen and unquenched.

Vaatasena cursed them, 'Ye that know neither sleep nor waking, I have come out of my prison this night to give you a sterile and unredeemed twilight.'

A secret policeman challenged Vaatasena, 'Who goes there?'

'Friend,' said Vaatasena.

'Who?'

'Bahuka, the Pimp.'

The secret policeman bowed low, 'I am a poor secret police-man. I shall be grateful to be of any service to your Eminence.'

He bowed again and turned to go. Vaatasena too went his way, but presently turned back and called after the man. The secret policeman approached, his hands stretched out in a conditioned reflex.

'I did not call you to give you your bribe,' Vaatasena said,'but to tell you something of consequence. Come and stand close to me. I deceived you on an impulse. I am not Bahuka the Pimp, and am no comrade of the Partisans or the Presidency. You wasted your courtesy on me, calling me my Eminence. I am a wage-soldier who threw away his weapon and fled the border, thirsting for his woman and his child. Do you understand, vermin?'

The secret policeman recoiled as from a venomous serpent. Vaatasena said, 'I lay my curse on you and your President, the vermin who sits on his pile of dung.'

The secret policeman drew his weapon and took aim; Vaatasena smiled 'Your guns are dead this night.'

The secret policeman pulled the trigger but the weapon slept, bound by the bondsman's sorrow.

'The guns of the class you serve,' Vaatasena said, 'will not go off this night. This is the night of the bondsman. Come close to me.'

Helplessly, the secret policeman obeyed.

'I feel no hatred towards you,' Vaatasena said.'In truth, my heart goes out to you.' And he took the man by the throat.

'Spare me, brother,' the secret policeman cried, 'I am innocent.'

Vaatasena strangled him and threw him into the gutter.

'There are no innocent victims,' he said.

Along the deserted paths Vaatasena walked in search of his woman and his child. He was tired when he reached his house; the doors were open and it was dark inside.

'Sunanda! Laavannya!' No one answered his call. In the yard

where the moonlight lay spotted like a leopard, Vaatasena rested for a while. The breeze was abrasive in his eyes.'Sunanda, my son, the night is advanced. Wherever you are, sleep!'

As he rose and walked on, he said to himself, *The bondsman's night is running out, and yet I have done nothing to destroy this city.* Through the avenues and the lanes, and the carnival spaces of the city, Laavannya's husband walked; he thought of her and his son no longer, he thought of nothing, but walked on, reaching tentacles out into the loneliness, an octopus which had grown a hundred tentacles of despair, swimming through a black sea.

'I curse this city," he said, his hundred tentacles raised in weird pageant,'I curse this country, every country that consigns its soldiers to wild frontiers. May the sovereigns of the earth rot away in my curse!'

He was now in a vast square, at the centre of which stood a marble statue. Vaatasena walked up to it.

'You!' he said, recognizing the likeness.'Vermin!'

It was a statue of the President's father.

'The founding father of Dharmapuri's pretences!' said Vaatasena, spitting on the statue pityingly, and scarring it desultorily with a piece of granite. 'Ah, you are but a statue. Were you not one, had you a living body, I would have shorn your genitals from it and destroyed your seed, because those that exercise power over their fellow-creatures have no right to procreate, nor do they deserve a requiem when they are gone.'

Vaatasena's mind was churning, it spilt into the moonlight and became madness. He spoke now in madness, in its innocence and truth and power, 'Braggart! Vermin! Had you saved a single child freezing on the sidewalks, it would have measured more in grace than a hundred of your vain perorations, and I might not have raved thus against your mute statue. But while you postured and preened, my class, deprived of nutrients for their bodies, begat blind progeny.'

From Vaatasena's eyes, as from the opaque pain of blind children, tears fell onto the cobblestones.

'No,' he said, clambering on to the statue, 'I have not come to break you. Because you never really lived, and so were a lie, you do not deserve even punishment. How shall I treat a lie? Perhaps, in this manner...'

Vaatasena squatted on the marble shoulders and defecated; the wage-soldier's dung flowed and stuck along the sculpted contours. Then in strange penitence Laavannya's husband moaned long like a beast of the forest. He climbed down from his perch and resumed his ghostly walk when he was stopped by a gentle touch on the shoulder.

'Who are you?' asked Vaatasena.

'Don't you remember me, sir? she said. 'Don't you remember Kaanchanamaala, Kanakalata's blind daughter? Why do you grieve, sir?'

'I grieve.'

'Why do you tire yourself, raging against a lie?'

'O Kaanchanamaala, I am a lie too. I who have held my weapon on a mountain side and wasted my years, I cannot be true, can I? I who had given up the loves of my body for that vermin's vainglory....'

He slumped to the ground, and, kneeling over him, Kaanchanamaala touched his body, caressing unseen injuries with the medicaments of the spirit.

'Arise, sir,' she said. 'You are no lie, you attained your truth when you cast away your weapon.'

'Is that true?'

'It is true indeed.'

Vaatasena rose, and Kaanchanamaala said,'Do not weep, sir.'

'O Kaanchanamaala, the pain of generations of wage-soldiers fills me.'

'Alas!' said Kaanchanamaala.'When I slept in my mother's womb they denied me nutrients, and fed their armies instead, and so I came sightless into this world.'

'Alas!' said Vaatasena. 'They fed their armies but not their soldier-bondsmen. We stood guard in wind and snow, and were shot dead in the gorges, or hit by the lightning on mountain peaks where we burned like torches.'

For a while both fell silent, then Kaanchanamaala spoke, 'Sir, seek out the Mendicant.'

'Is not the Mendicant dead?'

'He is not, they have him in prison.'

'God!'

'Go, sir,'said Kaanchanamaala.'Strange stars have risen tonight. This is the night of the bondsman. All the prisons lie open tonight. Go before they close again.'

Vaatasena limped forward, then turned. 'O Kaanchanamaala, you are the blind one who sees everything. Where is my son Sunanda?'

'Sunanda is far away,' she said 'on the banks of the sacred Jaahnavi.'

Vaatasena calculated distances and said, 'To the Mendicant's prison. From the prison to the banks of the Jaahnavi. Will I ever walk this distance? God, my God!'

'You will. Have no fear.'

'Will I see Sunanda?'

'You will,' she said.

'O Kaanchanamaala,' asked Vaatasena, hesitant, 'is the fever still on my son?'

'A great benediction has come upon Dharmapuri,' she replied. 'It has taken the fever away.'

'Benediction?'

'The grace of Siddhaartha.'

'Siddhaartha?'

'The King.'

Through the last hours of the bondsman's night Laavannya's husband sought the prison of the Mendicant.

CHAPTER XVII

The Stars Set

Along the unending paths Vaatasena wearily journeyed on; the great stars were now dipping westward.

Ah, thought the soldier-bondsman, *they set!*

Beyond the deserted sidewalks on either side, the shuttered shops· brooded, their facades cavernous shadows. In the dark Vaatasena heard the sound of panting. He stopped and listened. 'Who is there?'

The panting stopped, but soon began again.

'Who hides there?'

The panting came from behind a garbage dump. Vaatasena went round it to discover, crouching behind that precarious shelter, a teenaged girl of exceeding beauty.

'My child,' he said,'where are your clothes?'

'Sir,' the girl said,'use me as you choose to, but protect me.'

As Vaatasena pondered this, the girl went on,'I shall not resist, nor injure you. Nor do you need to struggle to rip my clothes away. Take me, sir, all I ask for is succour.'

The starlight gently picked its way over the contours of her nakedness: Vaatasena saw the tiny buds that were her breasts, and the blood clotted on her sinless thighs.

'Protect me,Sir.'

My child, my child, cried the soldier within himself, shaken by the sight of so little blood, by the combat of violence and innocence; he cupped her face in his palms and kissed her tresses.

'Take me, sir. I have not come of age, and hence know no lust. What you see on my thighs is the blood of rape; it has been done, and will hurt me no more.'

Vaatasena removed the cloak from his shoulders and wrapped

it round her. 'My child, who did this to you?'

Fear, and the sorrow of the shelterless, came over her and she remained mute; Vaatasena looked up again at the stars; he sensed the threatening dawn that lay in wait beyond them.

'Speak, my child,' he said, 'make haste.'

She came over and sat on his lap, and was a child again.

'Oh, sir, it was them,' she said, 'the police, and then the proletariat. Promise me, sir, that you will not deliver me into their hands again.'

Vaatasena consoled her with gentle words and touch, and as he felt her warm forehead, he thought in pain, *You are fevered, you too, my child.*

'And they are still chasing you?' asked Vaatasena.

She nodded and clung closer.

'But the proletariat,' said Vaatasena, 'why the proletariat?'

'I do not know, sir. My two playmates, Pramila and Shubhra, were caught earlier. They must be well on their way.'

'On their way? Where to, my child?'

'It is some mart of trade, sir. I know so little.'

'Children carted away to trading places? This is beyond the understanding of any bondsman-soldier who has spent his years scanning invisible frontiers.'

'Sir, I shall tell you what little I know. Time was when they shipped out only adult cadavers to the schools of medicine. But now they are hunting children; it is not for the schools but for another market.'

Again the panting seized her, and again, Vaatasena looked up at the setting stars.

'Beyond these stars is a remorseless dawn," he said. 'Make haste, my child.'

The dawn grew, a dark embryo hidden and faraway, wearing down the prophecy of the stars.

'I am Shaakuntala,' the girl said. 'Shaakuntala, the orphan. The hermits, gentle like the birds of the forest, looked after me.'

'And where are the hermits?'

'In prison.'

95

'Go on, my child.'

'After they took the hermits prisoners, they overran the hermitage.'

'God!'

'Sir, have I caused you distress?'

'Go on, my child.'

Shaakuntala continued, 'They overran the hermitage, and sought us out. They told us that we were merchandise, and raped us and put us in fetters. I alone escaped and hid among the plants of the garden.'

Now they heard an awesome rumble, which slowly drew nearer. Shaakuntala shuddered and rose from the soldier's lap and was gone. A crowd of men spilled down the road and moved past, their footfalls ebbing like the tributaries of a river carrying away the last dregs of the flood. Vaatasena looked up at the stars. Not all of them had set; he walked on again. At a crossing he was stopped by a crowd.

'Did you see the girl?' they demanded.

'Make way,' said Vaatasena.

'We are the proletariat,' they said, 'the risen prisoners of starvation. We toil in the gunneries, and in the workhouses packing cadavers. We demand our Surplus Value back, from the gunnery and the charnel house. We demand the democratization of the gun and cadaver trades, and workers' participation in the management of Sorrows. The monopolists keep stopping our Sorrows, the gunnery workers resent this. Whenever a Sorrow is ended, the gunnery workers ought to be compensated....'

'Workers of the gunnery,' Vaatasena said, 'I am a Persuader!'

'A Persuader!' the workers said.'A consumer of our product! We are delighted.'

'I am not. I have cast away my weapon, your product. I want none of your Sorrows, nor your prosperity. I spent an hour of my night grieving with a little girl. I ought to have spent it destroying your work houses. My time is running out. Make way!'

The proletariat's solidarity turned to rage.'A Persuader, who has abandoned the frontiers! Enemy of the machine and the revolution! Stop him!'

Vaatasena laughed aloud and said, 'Dim-witted ones! This is the bondsman's night. Make way!'

Vaatasena parted the crowd, like the prophet the sea waters, and walked on down the streets. His pace hastened, until he broke into a run, with the workers of the gunnery in pursuit. But he left them far behind, and their clamour was muted like the panting of the hermits' foundling. The stars were setting. ⁵Before the prisons close. Faster, faster!'⁵ Vaatasena sped on.

*

Vaatasena's legs felt numb; he fell and rose feebly and pushed on again until he stood before the great prison house. Stone walls and moats surrounded it, and the bars of its portcullis were pointed like spears. Standing before the portcullis, Vaatasena called out,'Mendicant Father, are you still inside? Tonight was the bondsman's night. Why did you not come out of the prison?'

Like a spring that wells out of a dark rock-crevice, an unspoken reply reached out to Vaatasena: *Look what a vast servitude surrounds this prison! But within these walls is the prison's truth and its freedom.*

The stars were setting, the bondsman's power ebbing away. Vaatasena asked, 'Mendicant Father, this was the bondsman's night. Why did you not destroy the gunneries?'

The unspoken voice said : *I spent this night in penance for the mis-spent freedoms of men.*

'Mendicant Father, you see with your mind's eye. Have they caught the hermits' foundling?'

My son, the unspoken voice replied, *We were the multitude, we were the chase. Now begone! Why did you this night destroy the peace of my incarceration?*

The portcullis rose. A pall of mist fell over Vaatasena's mind, and he listened to the rhythm of anklets. Shaakuntala stood naked before him, anklets of gold around her feet, her breasts grown large and her thighs cleansed and fair. She called out to Vaatasena, *Come to me, sir, the rape has been washed away, and I have become a woman.*

O Shaakuntala, Vaatasena said, *the night of the bondsman is ending, and I have accomplished nothing.*

Look on my breasts, sir, she said. *And my thighs, on the fair skin around my navel.*

My child! My child! Vaatasena cried.

Shaakuntala was over him, solid no longer, but a swirling, enveloping mist. In that great dissolution of touch, the anklets now exploding inside him, Vaatasena moved on to a tumultuous orgasm.

He fell across the doorway of the prison; inside the high turrets giant wheels turned on rusted axles, the portcullis descended again. Dimly Vaatasena remembered the bars of the portcullis looked like pointed spears. Now as they pierced his flesh, to the slow grind of the wheels, the last of the strange stars set, and the dawn broke, blind and menacing. The blood of the soldier-bondsman spilled over the cobbles, and grew cold.

*

Tides of water carried the blood away: the waters of the Jaahnavi, the river which leaves her celestial home and flows down to heal the souls of men. On the banks of the Jaahnavi, Vaatasena saw Laavannya and Sunanda.

The sun fell on Vaatasena's corpse. The guards freed it from the bars of the portcullis.

'A pity it is all pierced through,' they said.

'It cannot be shipped.'

'Truly a waste of exchange.'

'We can use its fat, which is about all. Send it to the soap factories.'

After the body was removed, the ants, in the ancient covenant of man and insect, came to lick away the clots of blood. In the blindness of that dawn, in the light of the prison, the Great Mendicant slept.

CHAPTER XVIII

The Old Ones

This tale of fantasy is deception, a length of burlesque worn around myself, beneath which lies my unremitting Sin. I interrupt the fantasy to stand bared before you for a moment, with this book in my hand, this book which I shall open for you. Here on this page is a picture of stripped women, heaped one on another, a baroque mound of bared anatomy the Jewesses of Auschwitz and Treblinka on whom I have gazed a hundred times with desire. Lust, not for one heap of bodies, but a hundred, a thousand, lust smouldering over the Holocaust! I see that you too must look, that your lust too has risen. So be it; we are all cursed alike, you and I, and the tyrant who sent these women to their deaths. Let me turn the pages for you: here an old man, in the Warsaw Ghetto, hands raised in supplication, silver stubble on his face, his mouth toothless, pleading. He is your father and mine, infirm and humiliated ancestor, weeping primate: he stands before this young soldier of the Reich, pleading, Son, let me live a little longer. But you, the soldier, have no ears for the pleading, you raise your gun and you kill him; now you are in the skies where the cries of children cannot reach you, and you unleash on Hiroshima and Nagasaki the flaming orgasm of the apocalypse. You have your reason, you have done it for your Motherland, your Class, your Book. Time after time, in country after country, this is repeated, and the old man with the toothless whimper pleads in vain, the child from the far depths of the city cries out in vain. Now we are the old men, we are the children, you and I, and our sons and our fathers raise their weapons against us. Son and enemy, citizen and invader, change and overlap; yet in all that relentless flux, pain and the killing always remain the residue. Let me now resume my tale of fantasy.

killing always remain the residue. Let me now resume my tale of fantasy.

*

In Shantigrama, in the hut of Shubhraka the washerman, his old parents lay paralysed with age and disease. Shubhraka came home that evening as usual, tethered his donkey to the tree-stump by the door, and went into the hut with the washing. In a corner of the one room which was all the hut had, sat Neelolpala, his wife, stirring a broth of pig's guts for the family. The room was heavy with the slow dying of the old ones, and the rancid smells of the washing and the guts.

Swethambara greeted his son, 'A hard day, was it?'

Shubhraka did not acknowledge his father's welcome. Its abjectness angered him. His glance fell on Neelolpala's breasts where she sat stirring the broth. *I want to disrobe Neelolpala, my woman,* thought Shubhraka, *and see her and make love to her in the arousal of that seeing.* A hate rose in him for all that thwarted his desire: the invalids, the stench of washing, and his own children. *I shall never see her naked in this room, and this is how I shall age and weaken into paralysis and pass away.* Shubhraka thought of the generations of washermen who had lived and died the same way: and he pitied his own parents Swethambara and Dhavalakeshi.

'My son,' Dhavalakeshi said, 'I see you are tired today.'

To this too he was silent.

'Son,' she said, 'have a bowl of broth.'

The inane solicitude, the ingratiating manner, the precarious clutch of the invalids. *God how they torture me!* Shubhraka thought. He turned away, cursed and spat, and the invalids listened in fear.

Wading through the fetid odours of the hut, Shubhraka stepped out into the street, where people, sad and stifled like himself, wandered desultorily, men who had never seen their women naked. The dusk grew heavy with their bitterness, its air too dense to breathe; once in a while a painted transvestite capered by, punctuating the dreariness with a burst of perfume.

As Shubhraka stood in the street, gazing after one of these transvestites, an Enumerator came by with a questionnaire.

'Your name?' the officer asked.

'Shubhraka, washerman.'

'Do you believe in the Celestial Birds?'

Shubhraka chanted slogans celebrating the Celestial Birds and the Sacrament, and presently the officer signalled him to stop.

'That will do. Now tell me if you are willing to help the Confederate Schools of Medicine and our own exchequer.'

'I am willing, sir.'

'How many are there in your house?'

Suddenly the spaces of Shubhraka's mind were filled with a naked and cavorting Neelolpala. His voice rose to a hysterical pitch,

'I have two to spare.'

He was afraid to lower his voice, afraid that its sin might sink like sediment into the crevices of his mind. He went on to answer the questionnaire, 'Swethambara, seventy years, and Dhavalakeshi, sixty-two.'

'Are they faulty of limb?' the officer asked.

'No, sir. They are paralysed but their limbs are whole and they will suit your purposes.'

'Good. The carrier will be here presently.'

From within the hut came the crying of the old man and woman; the hut filled with the wailing, as with the lust and anger of Neelolpala, who sat before the broth of pig's guts.

Shubhraka asked the Enumerator, 'How good are the prices?'

'There is a slump. Yet it is so much precious exchange.'

'That is not fair by the sellers.'

'Do not despair. New markets are opening up, new concepts of trading. Do you have children?'

'Two. Chandramukhi, fifteen years, and Dhrudhabahu, sixteen.'

'Good.'

'But I have no desire to sell them while this slump is on.'

'Be reasonable. Do you not realize the country is in a State of Crisis, and needs all the exchange it can lay hands on?'

Neelolpala leapt out of the hut, beating her breasts. 'You shall not take my children away! No one shall take my children away!'

Sullenly the neighbourhood listened. In another hut another woman stirring her broth of pig's guts told her husband, 'Let us go and see what is happening to Neelolpala.'

'There is no need for that,' said the man.

'It might be our turn tomorrow.'

'We shall do what we need to do when our turn comes. Now, sit down and stir the broth.'

Each hut became an island; in these isolations the men waited for their pots of broth to boil, and cursed the lamenting voice of the woman which called out for her children. When the lament became insistent, a few of them came grudgingly out of their islands and gathered in front of Shubhraka's hut. The Enumerator shouted at them, 'This assembly is illegal. Disperse!' And they slunk back, dispirited, to their huts.

Shubhraka said to the officer in anger and frustration 'What persecution is this! My father and mother destroy my peace with their wailing, and my mate frustrates me with hers. Tell me, sir, does not a man deserve to look at least once on the nakedness of his woman? Does he not deserve the privacy of his hut? Have pity on me, sir, and ship my parents and my children away, clearing for me the space of my hut. I want to light a lamp and see my woman in its dancing glow and then die. One must die thus, will you not agree with me, sir, even if one were dying for one's country?'

'Well and truly spoken,' the officer said.

'Buy all four of them, sir. Forget that I ever bargained with you. Nor do I mind the slump. All I want is the space of my hut. God, my God! Why does everyone hunt me down, and riddle me with guilt so that I lose the strength to sell may father and mother and the children I have begotten? Ah, I am a helpless little man and all I need is my hut and a lamp to see my woman by, all I need is this little hut and one night of love. After that I promise you, my gods, I shall make a pyre out of this washing, and immolate myself on it.'

'Collect yourself,' the officer said, 'the carrier is here.' A lumbering carriage drawn by black buffaloes drew up in front of the hut. Neelolpala stood in the doorway of the hut, barring the way, and the crying within the hut rose to a crescendo. The Enumerator was angry. 'Silence!' he commanded.

'Yes,' said the leader of a posse of armed men who suddenly appeared from nowhere, 'let there be silence.' They untied the buffaloes and freed the men and women who were bound inside the carriage. 'What do I see?' the Enumerator said, aghast.

'Persuaders destroying the merchandise of the nation!'

'We are not Persuaders,' the men said. 'We are the soldiers of Paraashara.'

The Enumerator was stunned by the reply, he looked at the soldiers as though they were apparitions; then shrilly invoking the Sacrament, he fled down the street. The black buffaloes bellowed and scattered. The children stepped out of the hut now, timidly, and came to their father. Shubhraka embraced them and wept. The people of the neighbourhood came out of their huts and stood around. Then in their midst appeared the Stranger.

'What goes on here?' asked the Stranger.

Chandramukhi and Dhrudhabahu answered together, 'Our father grieves.'

'Who are you, sir?' asked Neelolpala.

'Siddhaartha,' the Stranger replied.

'The King?'

'Yes.'

'O King,' said Neelolpala, 'where do we begin our story, where do we end? Of that we have no knowledge. It is a story which you will never understand.'

'I shall understand,' Siddhaartha said.

Neelolpala's lament rose thin like a silken thread and subtly it pierced the ears of the bystanders.

'King,' she said, 'we are the ones who wash away the stains of men.'

The moon rose full in the sky, and Siddhaartha led the woman to her husband, and the moon shone over her.

'Henceforth,' Siddhaartha said, 'you need not wash the stains and sweat away.'

The washerfolk asked him, 'King, who will do it if we do not? How will this city wear unstained clothes.'

Siddhaartha smiled and said, 'Let no one hide his sins with clothes.'

Down the street the noise of Paraashara's soldiers died away. Siddhaartha laid his hands on Shubhraka's and Neelolpala's shoulders. He disrobed them, and the man and the woman stood gazing at their bodies in the moonlight.

*

The journey began. The invalids rode the donkey, the children led the beast on, and following, Shubhraka and Neelolpala gave themselves up to love. Soon the street was behind them, and then the city. They walked on. Shubhraka and his wife asked, 'O King, where are you leading us?'

The King smiled and answered, 'Where there are neither stains nor washing.'

The convoy moved on behind Siddhaartha: the invalids in search of cleansing waters, the children celebrant, and the men and women in love. They walked on seeking the infinite peace of the Jaahnavi. Many others hearkened to the call and soon a multitude walked behind the King.

CHAPTER XIX

The Echoing Valley

The call travelled on, subtly insistent. It knocked on the nesting places of men, on their benumbed privacies.....

*

Kashyapa, the tradesman, was felling trees in the forest. He stood in his camp house and watched the saws at work in the valley below. Tree after tree fell, and from where he kept watch, on the rise of the plateau, each falling tree was a dimple in the green spread of foliage. Down in.the valley, the saws brought forth bursts of living tree dust and sprays of sap. Giant trees, patriarchs, fell with the noise of avalanches, and as they fell primordial shades were erased from the earth, and the dryads of the woods cursed the machines and flew to other *mandalas. The trees wailed, and their aged voices sought the listener on the plateau; Kashyapa stopped his ears with his palms; I cannot bear it any longer,* he thought, and called out to those who manned the machines,'Stop it! Stop the saws!'

The saws were stilled on the deep and bleeding gashes. Kashyapa spoke to his Keeper of Books, 'Chitragupta, what happens if we stop this felling?'

Chitragupta did not answer; he concluded his master was jesting. Yet when Kashyapa insisted, he said, 'Master, work will stop in our paper mills.'

'How many people work in those mills?'

'A thousand.'

'How many hands would it take to plant the forests again and raise orchards in the foothills?'

'An enormous work force, sir.'

'Our thousand workers can be happily employed.'

The master is jesting, thought Chitragupta, for no one in his right mind would stop the wheels of the workhouse, neither worker nor captain of industry. The jest took hold of Chitragupta, and he laughed; Kashyapa laughed, too, and he said, 'Laugh, Chitragupta! How long is it since we have laughed like this?'

Levity gave way to foreboding. Chitragupta said, 'How can I, master? I now see that you do not jest.'

'What else am I doing then? In this great green innocence of the forest I want to play.'

'Master, how can you close down the workhouse? Think of the wrath of the proletariat!'

'They will be angry, Chitragupta. The mill is the workers' vested interest much more than it is that of the owner.'

Consternation came over Chitragupta. Kashyapa went on, 'Tell me now, my friend, are you scared of fruits?'

'You speak in riddles, master.'

'You are indeed scared of the fruits that ripen on branches. That is why you eat them out of cans. Have you forgotten the feel of tree bark on your body as you climbed up to pluck the fruits? Your childhood, Chitragupta!'

'I have forgotten, master. Almost.'

'I shall revive your memories, Chitragupta!'

Kashyapa withdrew into the camp house, and Chitragupta stood outside, unable to comprehend the insanity that had seized his master. Presently, Chitragupta heard things being pulled down and ripped apart. Kashyapa was dismantling his chamber. Chitragupta peeped in to see Kashyapa tear away a priceless length of carpeting.

'Chitragupta,' Kashyapa said, 'the first ever carpets were woven by craftsmen imprisoned by invading chieftains.'

Kashyapa threw out the carpet, and after it, books of accounts and wads of currency.

'Master!' Chitragupta exclaimed, in dismay.

'We will be free of these. Look out over there, Chitragupta.'

'Where, master?'

'Out there are carpets of living grass. Look how the evening sun lights up their emerald. Have no fear, Chitragupta; step out on them unshod.'

Chitragupta, anger overcoming his awe of the master, spoke in reproach, 'You are destroying the books of accounts? You are going insane! You are turning into an enemy of the people!'

Kashyapa responded in a voice which Chitragupta had not heard before, 'Out of my way, exploiter, parasite!'

Chitragupta stood aside as his master heaped the carpets and the books and the currency into a pile, and set them on fire. The keeper of accounts, theologian of trade, looked on in terror as the flames enveloped his books. Tears filled his eyes as he watched the sacrilege.

'Stop, master! Listen to the voice of reason...'

'No, Chitragupta, my brother! My ears have no more room for your reasoning. They are filled with the wailing of aged trees, they are filled with the call of my King.'

More and more people listened to these voices; in Dharma-puri's sweeping reaches men quickened like seeds on which an unseen and magic rain had fallen; in the skies above, strange and menacing clouds sailed by and signalled those on the ground with spring thunder. Men broke out of their calloused husks in cleansed and ecstatic sprouting, and looked on sky and earth with joyous seedling eyes.

*

In this waking and seeing was treason. The masters of Big Wealth and the masters of Big Labour, the Princes of Trade and the Great Proletarians, and the Keepers of Books, hunted the traitors down.... Through the streets of Shantigrama, Jaralkaaru, a ten-year-old boy was led in fetters by policemen. School child-ren, lined up on either side of his route, clapped their hands and chanted rhythmically: *Death for spying! Death for spying!*

Walking through the crowd Siddhaartha sought out their teacher and asked him, 'Wise Preceptor, I venture to ask merely out of a desire to know...'

'Ask,' the teacher said.

'Where are they leading this child?'

'Child? Do you call him a child? He is Jaralkaaru the traitor, the spy of Imperialism.'

The child followed his captors, dragging his fetters along; his eyes full of the innocence of his age, he lifted his gaze to plead with his class-fellows lined on either side, but the children chanted what they had been taught to chant: *Jaralkaaru to the gallows! Jaralkaaru to the gallows!*

'What is his crime?' Siddhaartha asked.

'Treason,' the teacher said. 'A subject beyond the comprehension of the ordinary citizen. In truth, it is only the arrogant who would want to solve its puzzle.'

Siddhaartha persisted, 'Yet, Venerable Teacher...'

The teacher swore, and said, 'You waste my time, stranger.'

And saying this he closed his eyes, and pressing his fists to his temples, broke into a frenzied chant. Siddhaartha walked on, and after some distance he accosted a citizen. 'Citizen,' said Siddhaartha, 'Are they taking this child straight to the gallows?'

'You must be out of your senses to think so,' the citizen said.

'There are laws in Dharmapuri, and the traitor will be tried according to them.'

'You have not tried him yet. Why then do you call him a traitor?'

'O dull-witted one! We do so because he is a traitor.'

'Then why the seats of justice?'

'To implement the verdict of the people.'

'I do not understand,' Siddhaartha said, 'I do not understand.'

'Then get lost,' the citizen said. 'I have no time to waste on those who do not understand.'

And the citizen gnashed his teeth and began his chant. All down the street, from unseen alleys, the militant crowd clamoured for blood. Siddhaartha took in its myriad chants,

through which came the piercing voices of children:
Hang Jaralkaaru to fight poverty!
Hang Jaralkaaru to defeat the Imperialist armada!
Hang Jaralkaaru — Dharmapuri is in peril.

Siddhaartha followed the fettered prisoner, and thus reached the gates of the Hall of Justice, where the officers of the Law had positioned Jaralkaaru's parents and brothers and sisters in a surreal ensemble. As Jaralkaaru approached them, no longer did he chant out his guilt, or hold up his fetters in grateful patriotism.

'O, my father and mother,' he cried, 'do not let them kill me!'

For a long moment the lament of childhood swamped crime and punishment and patriotism, but soon the State of Dharmapuri swung round and rallied, and Jaralkaaru's parents and his brothers and sisters broke into a chant: *Death to the spy! Death to the spy!*

God, God! Siddhaartha thought, *this voice is alien.*

Jaralkaaru's parents and his brothers and sisters chanted on: *Death to Jaralkaaru! Death to Jaralkaaru!* The mother's voice rose shrill, *Death to the spy, death to my son!* spiralling into lunacy and terror; then she swooned and fell, and the crowd broke into hysterical applause.

Jaralkaaru entered the Hall of Justice, and after him, Siddhaartha. The officers of the Law marched Jaralkaaru's family into the chamber and lined them up in front of the Judge's desk. A herald of the Court read out the indictment, then the Judge addressed Jaralkaaru, 'Prisoner, do you have anything to say?'

The prisoner peered upward at the Judge, the prosecutors and the costumed heralds, avuncular presences round his death bed; no longer was he the star tragedian of the street tableau but a child of ten, and his captors mere childhood tormentors, apothecaries ministering to his terminal illness. He looked up at them and began to cry.

'O Jaralkaaru,' the Judge said, 'spy of Imperialism! Do you hear the voice of the people? It has condemned you. What am I, a mere judge, before the wisdom of the people? I am nothing

109

more than the instrument of their will.'

Now the knowledge dawned on Siddhaartha: the love of one's country demands the killing of children. The knowledge seared him like the sun at noon.

Siddhaartha sat in contemplation, with no *pipal* to stretch its merciful canopy overhead; and the Judge finished the last cantos of the judgement, and all round were the sounds of the people. The officers brought forth Jaralkaaru's mother, who had revived by then, and prompted her to chant. They walked Jaral-kaaru away to the cells of the condemned; a primordial cry rose within the mother, *My son! My son!* but its syllables, chiselled out by the pervasive evil, came out as the chant of slogans. The guardsmen cracked their whips, the guardsmen cried and sorrowed; even after all else had stopped, Jaralkaaru's kin kept up the chant.

God, God! Siddhaartha reflected, *what voice is this, which is not of man nor animal, neither of the mate nor of the offspring? I know now!* He listened with the seeker's alertness, and heard its echo down the centuries, through the dark valleys of memory. *It is,* Siddhaartha realized, *the eunuch voice of history!*

CHAPTER XX

The White Overlord

In the citadels of the earth's rulers the voice of history was the sibilant on the lips of the concubine, it was the goat-cry. The President rested in the stupor of a discharge, an august occurrence of state, while a concubine knelt naked, her head buried in his crotch; before them stood Pureeshananda, Dharmapuri's erudite Minister of the Interior.

'O elephant-gaited one,' the President said to the concubine, 'guess who stands before us, palms joined together prayerfully. He is the author of our Laws of Crisis, the architect of Dharmapuri's jurisprudence. Can you recognize him with his clothes on?'

'I can, my Lord,' the concubine said, smiling at the President's humour, for he had acquired her up from Pureeshananda's own harem. She looked up from the Presidential crotch, like a languorous serpent, her damp eyes half-closed, and her snake's tongue darting over sullied lips.

'Woman, in what fashion would you like to amuse yourself with this august personage?'

Neither the President nor the whore quite realized the enormity of the proposition; it was a call to play with the powers of the State, to play with history. Princes and Presidents played in erotic ritual for their concubines, they played thus while they reigned, in the little time they had, which they mistook for permanence. And they became playthings of their own evil, became toys which they knew must come apart and eventually disintegrate into rubble. Yet they played on, and warded off the terror with dalliance.

The concubine giggled softly and spat on the Minister's face.

Pureeshananda stood still, as the spittle trickled down his nose to his chin. The concubine winked at the Minister and laughed, and the President, infected by her merriment, terrorized Pureeshananda with a swear word.

'Vermin!' the concubine said, addressing the Minister.

'Yes, my Lady,' Pureeshananda said.

The play was becoming headier.

'Vermin,' the concubine said, 'goose-step in front of me!'

Helplessly the Minister raised his gaze towards the President; but the ruler of Dharmapuri gazed back with strange, grotesque eyes, the eyes of the cretin child preparing to molest the plaything. The Minister goose-stepped before the concubine, back and forth, like the men of his own constabulary, while she kept time like a metronome: 'Left, right, left, right....'

'Most stimulating coquette!' the President said, caressing her hair. The concubine squirmed on the President's lap, with many sinuous movements of her body; the President was no longer caressing, but tugging at her hair, which yet she took for loverly caprice. But the tugging became rough and insistent and she looked up; she saw the President's face had grown ominous and she cried out in fear. Pureeshananda, scholarly observer of schisms in the Palace, now made bold to pause in his goose-stepping.

'Who ordered you to stop,' the President hissed, 'you lickspittle?'

The Minister moaned and resumed his goose-stepping, whereupon the President relented, 'You may stop!'

Pureeshananda knelt in gratitude, and the concubine, in tears, stood aside from the throne. Then the President spoke to the Minister, 'Pureeshananda, we are well pleased in you. With great mastery over the empty word you have written out the Laws of the Crisis. Now, concubine-vermin, this high-serious converse is not for the likes of you; therefore, we command you to stop your ears with your palms.'

The concubine did as she was commanded, and the President resumed his converse of the state with the Minister, 'Pureeshananda, the Confederates, despite everything, send us striped candy and sweetened feed, the flavours of which are unknown to our confectioners. It was just as well that we wrote out the Laws of the Crisis, because the scribes of the Western media are trying to embarrass our Provider, the Great White Father, suggesting that we have regressed into a primitive lawless state. We might need better laws, and many more of them.'

'We will have them, sire,' Pureeshananda said. 'But let this nation rejoice meanwhile, because should our Imperialist providers fail us, there are always the fraternal Tartars to turn to. Their confectioners' collectives...'

The President flew into a great rage.

'Silence, vermin!'

Pureeshananda quaked with fear; the President went on, 'Do not speak of things you are ignorant of. Beside Confederate cookery what the Tartars might offer us is inedible, fit only for delegates to the Peace-and-youth jamborees. The Tartars themselves, when they come out of their country, hunger for the culinary art of the Confederacy.'

'This miserable one has been enlightened,' Pureeshananda said.

During this exchange, a white man had entered the chamber past the weakly protesting guards; the President and his Minister lost in high-serious converstopped were taken by surprise, but reflexes, conditioned through the centuries, caused them to bow down before the intruder.

'Venerable one,' the President said to the white man, 'from the sturdiness and magnificence of your limbs we make bold to guess that you must be a citizen of the Great White Confederacy.'

'So I am,' the white man said.

'What might you be, sire?' the President asked. 'A venerable spy, or a Captain of the Military-Industrial Complex which provides this humble one with candy?'

'Neither, I am a mere citizen.'

'Whatever you are, sire, we are honoured.'

The white man looked from the naked President to the naked concubine to the clad Minister. Now the President, smiling lewdly and ingratiatingly, propositioned. 'If it might please you, sire, we could bring her to you ourselves...'

The white man gazed at this power tableau of the new emergent peoples; the concubine grew seductive and bashful.

'Sire,' the President said, 'she is well versed in the art of love which, in this part of the world, our ancient civilization had perfected. My own Minister of the Interior will bring her to your suite.'

'I do not need her.'

The President's eyes now fell on the package the white man was carrying. 'O Provider, is that package sweetened feed, flavoured like nowhere else on earth?'

The concubine and the Minister eyed the package too and so did the guardsmen through parted curtains. The white man flung it towards the President, who caught it in his outstretched hands and, undoing the wrapping, began eating out of it greedily. In the *angst* of that eating he shat.

'What wretchedness!' the white man said. 'I shall splurge this mess all over the media when I get back home.'

The President sat up on his haunches, chewing and excreting, and raised his hands in supplication.

'Write if you must, O White Overlord,' he said, 'of the defecation, but spare us and do not write about the eating, for if you do so, we shall stand reduced in the eyes of the White world and may not be able to sustain our State of Crisis.'

'The President speaks truly,' said a voice from one of the pillars. The white man, who had heard the ancient legend of the man-lion*within the pillar, drew back with some anxiety.

'Do not be alarmed, sire,' the President said, 'It is no man-lion, but one of Your Grace's own countrymen, an operative of the Confederate Intelligence Agency. Inside all our pillars are

*The half man, half lion incarnation of Hindu mythology which sprang out of a pillar to slay a tyrant.

114

friendly and fraternal spies. Our food and armaments, our candy and guns, all that we have, are given to us either by your great country or the Red Tartar Republic. The two of you decide our wars and our peace. Then why, one might ask, are there spies in this country? Well, gracious sire, the presence of a large contingent of spies complements the ceremony of the State.'

There were joyous titters from within the pillars.

'See how pleased they are,' the President said. 'The majority of the pillars hold men from the Confederate Intelligence Agency. Next comes the Red Tartar Intelligence. In the remaining pillars hide sundry spies from the wild countries.'

The white man kicked the pillar which had spoken first, causing the implanted spy to cry out in pain. 'Morons of the Intelligence!' the white man said in disgust. 'Living off the tax-payers' money like termites within these pillars! It is time my people knew of this.'

The pillar pleaded in alarm, 'Do not expose us further, sir. The media causes havoc enough, so do the Congressional Committees.'

'True, White Overlord,' the President added in support of the pillars. 'And it would be an act of disloyalty for you to expose your own country's network and its agents who through the mastery of occult arts of espionage have got themselves into these pillars. We in Dharmapuri cherish the presence of the Confederate Intelligence Agency. Even this humble one, taking brief respite from affairs of state, does occasional stringing for it, and for the Tartar Intelligence as well, to be true to our creed of neutrality.'

'President-Vermin!' the white man swore.

'Sire!' said the President, coming to attention.

The ruler of so large a country, the white man said to himself, *the master of majestic rivers, of mountains with their veins of gold, and of people and their inexhaustible power! Behaving like this!*

'White Overlord, sire!' the President said. 'Protect our State of Crisis!'

'Protect!' said the termites in concert, their eerie endorsement going round like echoes in a whispering gallery. The President prostrated himself before the white man, which threw his behind into relief. The sight of that behind, with its scab of excrement, terrified the Imperialist, and he beat a hasty retreat.

CHAPTER XXI

The Eyes of the Jaahnavi

Laavannya and Sunanda sat by the riverside and grieved over Vaatasena's death; their lament rose from the springs of the river and flowed on with its tides.

'Siddhaartha,' Laavannya said, 'what else did you see in your vision?'

Siddhaartha said, 'The Mendicant. I saw him in his prison cell. I saw Vaatasena's tortuous journey to that prison, and his death on the spikes of its portcullis.'

A calm enveloped Laavannya, and her lament, now silent, flowed through the subtle spaces within. On the moss of the river bank sat the King, quietly feeling the lament's tides of silence. Above them the jewels of the sky grew refulgent with prophecy, and Siddhaartha lifted his seer's gaze towards them.

'O Siddhaartha,' Laavannya said, 'what more?'

'It was the Night of the Bondsman,' Siddhaartha said, 'and I saw through the prison walls. I saw the Mendicant, saw the light in his eyes slowly turn to the glint of insanity.'

'God, merciful God!'

'And as that night of grace ended, they killed the Mendicant.'

Laavannya grew prayerful, washed in the blood of parricide. 'I cannot bear this, my King. What do the gods scheme for us?'

Siddhaartha did not reply; he looked up again at the orbits of the jewels and the beneficent mist. Laavannya no longer sought to know; sleep came over her, and trusting the King to know for her, trusting and surrendering, she rested her head on his lap. Siddhaartha gently laid her on the moss, and rose and walked down the river bank.

He had walked some distance when someone accosted him

from the shadows of the groves.

'You, Paraashara!' the King said, surprised.

'The Mendicant is dead...' the General said.

Siddhaartha smiled sadly. 'You have come back!'

'I have.'

'You are weary. Rest your limbs awhile.'

'My limbs, my King? But where shall I rest my spirit? They have killed the Mendicant.'

'I know. I knew of Vaatasena's death as well. I knew of the bondsman's night.'

'You knew, did you?' Paraashara said, bitterly. 'We shall avenge them.'

Siddhaartha laid a hand on Paraashara's shoulder. 'You are weary, Paraashara. Rest.'

'I cannot, I am full of revenge.'

'Paraashara,' Siddhaartha said, in great love, 'you err.'

'What then would you have us do? Give up?'

'Have you not known it, Paraashara? There is no defeat in our war, and no avenging.'

'My mind is weary, more than my limbs.'

'Come,' Siddhaartha said, and led the General by the hand down the riverside. The stars and the crescent moon gently lit the forms of the sleeping woman and child. Siddhaartha laid his palm on Paraashara's eyes.

'Look again, O Paraashara,' Siddhaartha said.

A great sorrow of seeing came over Paraashara, then a deeper consolation, as he looked again on the woman and the child. Paraashara saw genesis and love, he saw the slender thread which held together the plenitude of created things.

'I shudder, O King,' he said. 'I see that God resides in every despair.'

'You are fortunate. Now go to the woman and child, and rest beside them, while I walk these paths awhile.'

Paraashara did as he was told, and Siddhaartha, awaking within himself to the Bodhisattva's vigil, paced the lonely riverside. The river winds filled with hymnal voices, and the tides grew mystic, articulate; Siddhaartha knew the imminence of revelation.

As he walked, great clouds swept into his mind; beneath them the river darkened, and the darkening tides flowed over Laavannya. Siddhaartha walked on; he was on a pathway which stretched into enormous distances, and above him the skies hung low, a canopy of gathering rain. He saw Sunanda, a stranger now, seated all alone in this menacing desolation.

'Ah, my child,' the King grieved, 'why do you sit thus beside this path?'

'This is the pathway of the destitutes,' the child replied.

'On one side is the barren rise of the mountain, on the other the chasm, and overhead the clouds within which slumber fire and thunder.'

The child did not answer, but sat stooping over his beggar's bowl.

Siddhaartha walked on and after a while entered a strange city. He saw the child again, walking before him. The child, his body bruised and bleeding, said, 'I flee from the huntsmen. I am in pain.'

The King grieved, 'Do you have no one, my child? No one to make your pain their's?'

Siddhaartha woke out of the vision as he heard people by the riverside. He saw two dead Persuaders and a third in his death throes. An armed Paraashara stood guard over them. Siddhaartha called out, 'Laavannya, Sunanda!'

'They have been taken,' Paraashara said.

Siddhaartha stood silent a long while; Paraashara said, 'Wake up, my King.'

'I am awake, Paraashara.'

'I am going away.'

'Where?'

'I go in search of my arms and my soldiers.'

'Are you displeased in me, Paraashara?'

'No, my King. I despair because the grace you gave me has ended. And I seek once again the path of war.'

Siddhaartha's gaze went over the river, over the dead Persuaders and the dying one, and over the bed of grass where the woman and child had slept a little while ago.

'Go, Paraashara,' Siddhaartha said, 'and may good befall you.'

Paraashara stood still, palms joined, prayerful. 'Master, are you bidding me depart?'

'You have chosen the path of war once again. Yet our paths will meet.'

Paraashara spoke no more, but sadly turned away. Siddhaartha watched his stooped form recede along the river into the mist of the valley. He stood long after the General was gone, then walked to the river and called out in deep anguish, 'Ye gods of the river valley!'

Nothing moved save the waters of the river; Siddhaartha spoke into the night, *Why did I leave my kingdom? Why is Paraashara taking up arms again? Why did these men die, and why did they take the woman and child captive?*

Siddhaartha asked again, *Why do men turn away from the bed of love and the consuming pyre to garner wealth and rule over nations?*

And again, *How many more ages? How many more incarnations? How many more unfulfilled covenants?*

Siddhaartha said, 'Speak to me, I am in pain!'

Nothing moved, save the river. The celestial chariots cruised no more, and the jewels grew dim. Siddhaartha waited.

Then in the distance rose the stirring of heavy anklets and then, the rhythm of painful steps. Gigantic crowns of gold came into view, rough-cut gems and scarabaeid shells gleaming dully on them, and numberless hands holding up fabled weapons. The gods of the river valley, in mournful pageant, lined the bank. Siddhaartha looked at them and grieved. *Beloved deities,* he said, *without the incense of worship, without the fires of offering, what pallor has come over you, what enfeeblement and distress!* From the gods who knew the Bodhisattva's grief rose a deep wailing like the wind of the night. Siddhaartha said, 'Give me an answer!'

The gods of the river valley plucked out their eyes, and in serene rite, flung them into the current; in this way they answered the King. Like the purple fruit of the *jumbu* the eyes sank into the clear water, they became the black fish of the river, the moving eyes of the Jaahnavi.

O Siddhaartha, said the Jaahnavi, *with these eyes I see the far ocean, I see its enveloping blindness.*

Where their eyes had been were now anguished discs of black, and with these the gods looked on Siddhaartha. Then they turned and walked away, the sound of anklets fading into the valley.

CHAPTER XXII

The Whore and the General

Paraashara gathered his men and arms, and soon a great army marched under his flag; it came down the mountain slops and swept over the plains. City after city fell before it, and whole satrapies surrendered without resistance.

*

Minister for Sorrowing and defender of the Presidential throne, crawled naked at the feet of his wife, Priyamvada.

'What do you want of me, scullion?' Priyamvada asked.

In Hayavadana's loins and on his thick, wet lips a dull lusting hurt like a festering sore. When he importuned her again, she swore, upon which he wet the carpet.

Priyamvada bent over the carpet, and said, 'Vermin, you have sullied my carpet. It was a gift from your predecessor Rumannuaan.'

She paused in remembrance of days gone by, and came back to the stain on the carpet. 'Despicable vermin,' she soliloquized. 'One raises one's voice and they piss or shit. Perhaps it is only such vermin who can exercise hegemony over men.'

She rose, and raised her goblet of wine to her lips; then as her guts churned, she smashed the goblet over the patch of urine.

'Ah, but why blame this scullion, this cook's catamite?

Rumannuaan made me this gift for an afternoon's messing. The old man held me, and not knowing what to do with me, spilled over my navel and crotch. Stains! ' She broke into savage laughter..

'It is fitting that you, catamite-vermin, should in turn stain

Rumannuaan's carpet.'

Priyamvada picked up another goblet, and yet another; she reached for things made of rare and sculpted crystal and smashed them all. A vast heap of priceless glass grew on the carpet. Then she ripped apart her clothes and tore her tresses, and stamped and danced on the urine and the rubble. Hayavadana first dazed by her nakedness, and then aroused, circled her sheepishly.

'Do not dare touch me, scullion!' Priyamvada screamed.

Suddenly she stopped stomping about; tantalizingly and wickedly, she held out her big toe to the creature grovelling before her in imbecile lust. Kneeling, the Minister of Dharmapuri's armies took the toe into his mouth and sucked it. The sloshing on her toe quietened her frenzy, but then, at the sight of Hayavadana's behind, a woman's behind misendowed on a male body, she retched and vomited over its protuberances.

The bells of the speaking machine rang; 'This is from the Palace,' the caller said.

'Salutations!' said Priyamvada, wiping the vomit from her mouth.

'The President desires the presence of the Minister for Sorrowing,' the caller said. 'For consultations.'

'He shall be there forthwith. Praised be the Sacrament!'

She replaced the receiver on its cradle and spat on it. Turning to Hayavadana, she said, 'Go! the old satyr is calling you. To discuss the border wars, you know what that means.'

The rage was upon her again, and to Hayavadana, who had given up her toe and was circling her once more, she said, 'Go, my husband, to *yours*. Go, my little whore!'

His eyes blank, his lips slavering, Hayavadana kept up his sullen orbiting.

'Go!' Priyamvada said. 'The nation calls.'

Just then there was a loud and insistent knocking on the door. Even as Priyamvada was cursing the guardsmen for neglecting their duty, the door was flung open and a soldier entered. Hayavadana, surprised, turned on him, palms sheathing his tumescent organ.

'What obscenity!' the soldier said.

'Mutiny!' the Minister for Sorrowing said.

'What does this impudence mean?' Priyamvada demanded.

'I am a commando of Paraashara's, the soldier said, and a hush fell on the chamber. Even the guardsmen who had arrived to eject the intruder stood petrified. The soldier raised a hand in a gesture of command, 'I come to herald the General.'

Bugles and trumpets sounded outside and Paraashara entered, flanked by his aides. Paraashara asked, 'Are you Hayavadana?'

His hands still round his quickly shrinking erection, Hayavadana answered, 'The Minister for Sorrowing.'

Paraashara's eyes blazed with anger, and Hayavadana shat a little and let go his collapsing member. Paraashara spoke to Priyamvada, 'Forgive me, Lady, if I am rude.' And turning again to Hayavadana, he said, 'I asked you your name. Answer me!'

'Your pardon, General,' Hayavadana said, standing naked and shrunk before Paraashara.

'Hayavadana of the lush lips, are you not?'

'The Minister for Sorrowing.'

'Impudent moron!' Paraashara said, and Hayavadana shat again.

'Yes, my Lord,' Hayavadana said, 'Hayavadana of the lush lips.'

As he said this, the grotesque coyness of a whore came over the Minister for Sorrowing.

'Scullion, illiterate, minister,' Paraashara said, 'are you not all these?'

'Yes, my Lord. Scullion, illiterate, minister.'

Hayavadana's wife now stepped forward. 'Ignore him, General,' she said, 'and talk to me. I shall enlighten you. It is the likes of my dear husband here who seize sovereign power and wage wars, and use the lives of men and women. May your insurrection triumph, Paraashara!'

And she clasped Paraashara to her and kissed him on the mouth.

'Ah, a little fragrance here,' she said, 'punctuating the tyranny of excrement! A little valour amid crawling catamites!'

Slowly Paraashara disengaged himself, and said, 'My Lady, I must go.'

'I know you must, for your insurrection calls you.'

'I seek your forgiveness, for I have come to take your husband prisoner.'

Hayavadana moaned in terror, 'Mercy, O Priyamvada! Do not let them take me away.'

'They have come for you,' she said. 'Go now, little whore.'

The soldiers led Hayavadana away. Paraashara was now sad, his words faltered. 'Fair one, with great regret I consign you to loneliness.'

'Feel no guilt,' Priyamvada said. 'For I go to where there is no loneliness, to the streets where the whores live. I have been a leader of the State, and have had enough; the act is over, and now I become a whore again, back in the cages of my sisters.'

'We shall throw open the cages...'

Priyamvada grew sad, 'Varied are our perceptions of freedom, O Paraashara! And so are our paths; never might you understand me, for I grieve for my mothers, the ones who died in the cages and knew no justice. I shall not desire justice for myself.'

Hearing her say this, Paraashara despaired. He said, 'My mind fails me, Priyamvada. Tell me what I should do now.'

'My mind fails me too. But this I will tell you: accomplish whatever you have set out to.'

'I took up arms, defying the wishes of my King.'

'Then fight well. And I, ah, the cages beckon me.'

'It was in the same way that the Mendicant refused to leave his prison. The Mendicant triumphed.'

'So does Siddhaartha triumph,' Priyamvada said.

Paraashara looked at her, baffled, then lost himself in her embrace again. Around them triumphs and martyrdoms withered away; her touch and scent enveloped him, and he desired her.

'Alas, my General,' she said, 'you have come a day too late.

Till yesterday I had my dreams of love, but from now on I am a woman of the cages. Have you sinned with a whore before?'

'I have not.'

'Then stay untainted. Our paths are different, and yet they might meet again.'

'So the King said to me.'

Go, my General. And God's peace be with you.'

Paraashara left, and Priyamvada listened to the fading tread of his soldiers. She stood a long while in contemplation of what had once been her home. Then, seizing a weapon from a guardsman, she stepped out into the night. The terror of the insurrection had kept the people indoors, and nothing moved save the shadows of tree branches, attenuated and ghostly, thrown on the sidewalks by the street lamps. Beyond the shadows, on either side, the mansions of the rulers loomed large and sombre. Priyamvada walked on, to the fringes of the city where the harlots' cages lay.

CHAPTER XXIII

Tinsel on the Coffin

In his bed of many loves, the President lay and ruminated, and the clangour of the State-the Persuaders and the deserting commander, the wars and the insurrection grew-distanced. The President spoke to himself in the silence that lay about him. He said, *Ah, my vital member sags like a worm, and on it are ageing calluses of disease. Who am I that cower behind this worm?* Deep within him a worm wriggled. *You are Pippalaada,* said the worm. Pippalaada! The name his unwed mother had given him, the name he bore as a citizen-destitute. It tore the lid off the dismal privacy of history. *Do not despair,* said the worm inside, *we are one person, you and I.* The President writhed in fear and pain, and he said, *No, no! I am the President, the reigning citizen.* The worm inside him laughed, *You are Pippalaada the worm. You ward off Pippalaada in vain; you do so with your palace and your armoury and your glittering ceremonies, but the worms of the nether earth call you, and soon it will be time for you to give yourself up to them.*

In fear the President called out, 'Pippalaada!' and the Palace maid sleeping beside him stirred awake.

'My Lord,' she said, 'did you call?'

She was fully awake now, and regarded the President with some alarm. 'My Lord, you do not look well.'

'What is your name, woman?' the President asked.

'Chitrangada,' she said.

'Have you been in bed with me before?'

'During the last five summers this humble one has had the good fortune only thrice.'

'Good fortune?' the President demanded. 'Do you call it good fortune?'

'My gracious Lord! What more may a woman desire?'

The President mopped the sweat from his forehead. 'I am a worm,' he said, like a peevish and insistent child. 'Does not the worm repel you?'

Chitrangada repeated what generations of her sisters had said in captivity, the ancient lie of the odalisque. 'Most gracious Lord! You fill me with desire.'

He hit her across the mouth. Her lips bled.

'Go from my sight,' he said.

The President saw her behind as she walked away; lust rose in him, and despair. The despair became the loneliness of the sovereign, the desolation of the lust of power. The bed stood under its canopy of silk and gold, at the heart of the jewel-spangled chamber, alone, insane. *There is no one beside me,* lamented the President, *there is no one! Where are the maidens' clasps of love, where the touch of children?*

'Where is my Secret Agent?' he screamed.

Ever present in the wings, the President's Principal Secret Agent stepped in and awaited his pleasure. The sight of the Secret Agent, discreet keeper of his fears, brought on a surge of tenderness within him; an anxious question formed inside his mind, which the Agent read but awaited in silence. At last the President spoke, 'What is the mood of the people?'

'My Lord,' the Agent said, 'the people revel in their prosperity, and the Birds minister to the destitutes...'

The Agent spoke on in sad ritual, as agents from time immemorial have spoken to their sovereigns. The President pretended to listen, and as the Agent went on and on, stopped him gently and without anger. 'Depart from my presence, brother.'

When the man was gone, the President called to the guards-men of the chamber again, 'Bring me the assassins.'

The assassins entered and bowed and the President enquired, 'have you finished Paraashara?'

The assassins panicked, but the President put them at their

ease.

'Speak without fear.'

They fell on their knees and grovelled, 'Have mercy on us, Lord! We have not yet got him.'

The President shook as if with ague, he beat his head and breast. The assassins spoke in dread. 'Like a fish in water, Paraashara loses himself among the people.'

'What futility, what waste!'

'Mercy, O Lord!-Your Grace will not find us wanting: we have consigned to highway accidents a thousand people on whom your displeasure has fallen.'

Hearing this the President raised a lament. 'Alas, you have burdened my futility with sin!'

The offering of a thousand deaths lay before his seat of power: the President tried to take in those thousand deaths, but their pain loomed large and grew beyond his knowing. He had the assassins whipped, and dismissed them, and called in the Wise Old One of his Court.

'Ancient One,' said the President, 'I read malignant signs, I fear. I cannot comprehend a thousand death-rattles; why do they not forgive me? What needs have I? A little candy and sweetened feed, a few concubines to rest my sorrows in.' As he spoke, the President was lost in pity for himself, the enthroned destitute. He went on, 'Will a thousand death-rattles throw me off my throne? Will my organ become a dried relic, as moths are transformed inside tomes of history? What a waste! Spies, assassins, scholars, seats of learning, shrines of worship... All wasted.'

The President wept in rage and self-pity. The Wise Old One bowed, and said, 'Come with me, my Lord.'

He led the President out of the chamber, then out on to the terraces; he wound his way up the minarets of the Palace. The President followed. He looked up at the sky, in fear of its infinite reaches. The moon shone, and so too the planets and the larger stars. The Wise Old One dug into his satchel, took out a fistful of gems, and laid them out on a slab of stone.

'These are soothsayers, sire,' he said. 'Soothsayers asleep. The sleepless ones are above, the jewels of the sky who travel along ceaseless orbits, carrying their burden of prophecy.'

The President looked up.

'Ask them,' the Wise Old One said, 'and they will answer.'

The President scanned the mists, his eyes hurt, and he said petulantly, 'Where are your jewels of the sky?'

'If you cannot see them, My Lord, it ill beseems me to read them for you.'

'Bear with me, Old One. I cannot see far, my eyes smart. ⁵You⁵ ask and get me the answers.'

'I have done so, Lord. Many times.'

'And what did they say?'

The Wise Old One smiled. 'That there are neither questions nor answers, only change and becoming. And one's own hour of passing.'

The President asked angrily, 'Do they say that I will change and go?'

I, the orphan child, hunted down the years, down the paths of abasement, I, who have reached this fugitive seat of power. God, God, do I have to go? With great kindness the Wise Old One read the President's thoughts, and grieved for the orphan-tyrant.

'My Lord, what a wealth of sorrow was yours, which you have direly wasted!'

The President swore bitterly, and the old man bowed in deference.

'Ungrateful one!' the President said. 'How shall I punish you for thus defiling my grief?'

The Wise Old One stood smiling; the President seized him and flung him down from the minarets into the darkness below, onto the silt of the moonlight. The President looked down, scanning the silt, and thought, *I can see nothing, neither the jewels of the sky, nor the sediments of the moon; on these terraces of my Palace, why does my seeing flounder?*

He descended, angry; through the stairways and corridors of his Palace he ran gasping, until he reached his chamber where he sought refuge in his bed. But a serene voice pursued him,

130

the voice of the Ancient One who had disappeared like a dim meteor into the silt of the moon. The voice called out to him, *O Pippalaada! Do not pursue me thus,* begged Pippalaada.

Look again within yourself, said the meteor's voice. *You can see the jewels of the sky there, and read their prophecy.*

But, Wise One said Pippalaada, *my eyes tire and dim. Now I am a blind child like Kaanchanamaala.*

Alas, Pippalaada, said the voice, *Kaanchanamaala sorrowed over the unwritten palm leaves of her childhood. You gave yourself no such redemption.*

Save me, sobbed Pippalaada.

How can I? said the voice. *You have denied your spirit the Way. How can I restore it?*

It grows dark, said Pippalaada. *What is this crypt that surrounds me?*

You were a dead man through the years of your reign, said the voice. *These confines are the boards of your coffin.*

Pippalaada wailed. *Where is my throne, where are my armies and my heraldic emblem?*

The voice of the meteor answered, *My son, hidden beneath the heroic tinsel was your coffin, and inside it, a mouldering fistful of earth.*

*

The swoon passed, and waking, the President looked round at the servitors and men of medicine ministering to him. Yet even in the daylight his eyes met the paved walls of the crypt; tiredly his glance shifted from face to face until it rested on Chitrangada, the maid. He signalled for everyone except her to leave the chamber.

'Chitrangada,' he said, his voice timorous.

'Yes, my Lord.'

But the President said nothing; after a long silence he said again, 'Chitrangada.'

'I am here, my Lord.'

131

'I hurt you.'

'Speak not thus, my Lord.'

The President sat up in bed and faced her. The sensual fullness of her body disturbed him no more. He saw her lips bleeding still, and touched them in remorse.

'Chitrangada,' the President asked, 'do you have a husband?'

'I do, my Lord,' said Chitrangada. 'He is Your Grace's ostler.'

The President gazed a long while at her lips, on the glistening wet of the sibilants smothered on them, the sound of his ostler's love. He sorrowed over the desecration. Over the wet of her lips she spoke, 'Do not grieve, my Lord, all this is yours....'

He silenced her with a finger laid across her lips.

'Chitrangada!'

'My Lord?'

'Do you have children?'

'A girl, sire. A nurseling.'

In sombre knowledge of the answer the President asked, 'Can she see?'

'No, my Lord. She is blind.'

The palm leaves are not for this nurseling, thought the President, *nor the* Khas *and the* Ghas, *the magic consonants of childhood.* Pippalaada, President, rose and drew the maid towards him. Her breasts filled with milk, a fullness she had not known before; the milk spilled like the tears of the blind nurseling. Pippalaada stroked her breasts, then her sides, and sank to the floor as his legs gave way.

Chitrangada lamented: *O blind progeny! O ancestors kneeling and groping in blind death-sleep!* She cupped his face in her palms and raised it to her breasts; the hour of motherhood filled the coffin. Pippalaada wept on the breasts; the tears fell on the mould and earth, and leavened them for the sprouts of rebirth.

CHAPTER XXIV

The Forests

As Paraashara marched into province after province, their cities surrendered, and their workhouses gave up, shutting the chutes that spewed slime into rivers; the river spirits rejoiced. And the forests rejoiced, their green corridors resonant with the ascetics' canticle, and their canopies resplendent with the celebrant lace of rain and lightning. Yet the core of Dharmapuri held out, and both the Red Tartar Republic and the White Confederacy backed the President with guns and aphrodisiacs.

A new and weird solidarity had begun to link the white and the coloured continents. This was an atavism which drew the White races once again into the primitive hunt for food. Foraging in land and water and mining on inert planets far away, in a misery greater than the deprivations of Dharmapuri, in a misery of turbulent skill and invention which left them unsatiated, they turned on their own kind. In the coloured world were teeming numbers, and in the white one, wealth and the turbulent appetite; the two worlds now sought to complement each other as in a mathematical equation. White demographers exhorted their brown and black brethren to beget more children, and gave them antigens and nutrients to ensure the babies were born soft and succulent. The age of empire lay behind them, an age of folly; the white brother came no longer to conquer, nor to baptize and educate; he came now to nurture and to *farm*.

The voice of the Mendicant, disembodied, went out to the men of the New Alchemy: *Turn back, my children! You have strayed far from the shores of compassion.* But the greedy sea wind filled their sails, as it had done in the ages gone by; there was no returning.

*

Pippalaada awoke. In the daylight the penitent images were gone: the shrill-voiced meteor, the moon-silt and the blind nurseling. Pippalaada sat up once again on his glittering catafalque. His first decree of the morning banished Chitrangada from the Palace; she would soon be dead on a highway, run over by a chariot. Thus was expiated the bittersweet suckling, and the President, reigning sovereign once again, immersed himself in the affairs of state. He summoned Shakuni, his Personal Envoy, and spoke to him, 'This new Sorrow of ours is not faring as well as it ought to.'

'Oh these Sorrows,' the wizened and cynical Envoy yawned, 'one blends with another, friend blends with enemy. But then, my Lord, between the two of us, need we speak of *Sorrows?*'

'Shakuni, Evil One,' the President said, 'if you too revile that word, what will become of us?'

Shakuni smiled. 'Then I shall not. Be at peace, my Lord.'

'This new Sorrow of ours is floundering. I implore you, O Evil One, to devise means of saving it.'

A maid entered, bearing a trayful of flavorsome food, human-flesh dressed as sunflower and fruit.

'Ah,' Shakuni said, 'we sell this meat. Since when has the comprador become consumer?'

A silence intervened, and was broken in their minds by faraway dirges, by brown mothers crying for children who had become meat, become sunflower and fruit. Shakuni sliced a portion daintily and raised it to his mouth; the room was filled with the heady smell of the flesh. Shakuni asked, 'Has this become a standard course in Palace cuisine, my Lord?'

'The men of science say this will help me regain my vitality.'

'That calls for rejoicing. Should your organ harden and rise, I, like any other citizen, would feel uplifted. After all, what is all this war and massacre for, but to facilitate your fornications? The masters of political science know this. However...' Shakuni paused and continued, 'However, in the minds of the people you are still an eater of cabbage and lettuce. That being so, the man-flesh must be kept a secret.'

'It is indeed a secret.'

'That is too comforting an assumption, my Lord. Every day, on a rough reckoning, three or four maids and concubines and an equal number of ministers' wives come to you. They have husbands and lovers, who in turn have concubines and women of casual amusement, who have lovers...'

The President pressed his palms to his forehead in anxiety.

'Shakuni, what are you saying?'

'I was merely saying,' Shakuni said, 'that the most strenuous censorship cannot hide all our secrets. Let me compute the number of people with whom you will share a secret should one concubine be privy to it.'

Shakuni pulled out an adding machine. 'Three times three is nine, nine times nine is eighty-one, and eighty-one times eighty-one is six thousand five hundred and sixty-one, six thousand five hundred and sixty-one times...'

The President shat.

In a feeble voice the President said, 'Call in my experts in reckoning.'

'To what purpose?'

'To save me from these figures.'

Shakuni clapped his hands and a guardsman looked in.

'Let the wizards of tallying stay back,' Shakuni said. 'Call in the scavengers instead.'

The scavengers came in and scooped away the excrement. After them came maids burning incense. The defecation had not relieved the President's anxiety. He sat paralysed, while his fevered brain pursued a relentless calculus; adding, subtracting, dividing and multiplying, erring and erasing and postulating again, he built over his head a mushroom of madness.

'Figures, Shakuni!' he said. 'I want to know the figures. How many people have by now known the secret of my infirmity?'

'Pippalaada, worm!' Shakuni said. 'Why do you experience shame? That emotion does not become the ruler of

Dharmapuri.'

'Ah, everyone will come to know...'

'Let them. Does it make a difference? There will be no street gossip, our police will take care of that; no newspapers will write about it. And you can, meanwhile, get the scribes to produce volumes of commemoration, hide-bound and gilded, and cast your likeness in bronze; behind all that historical rubble your worm will find refuge.'

'I will not die!'

'Eat your meat, and hold your tongue, fellow!'

And Shakuni fell to his own meal of human sunflower. 'Do not defecate again,' he said. 'I want to finish this delicious meal in peace.'

The President reddened in anger, 'Shakuni, vermin!'

'My Lord?'

'You speak to me without reverence.'

Shakuni laughed, 'How do you propose to punish my irreverence, my Lord?'

'I will sentence you to death.'

'That is all?'

'Right away,' the President said, and clapped his hands for the guardsmen. When the guardsmen entered the chamber, Shakuni motioned them away.

'Alas!' the President said. 'Even my henchmen obey you. O Evil One, may your progeny be blighted!'

Shakuni, connoisseur, went through his meal with delicate relish, and licked his lips in requiem for the minced child that had turned into sunflower.

'Pippalaada,' he said, 'have you forgotten? Try and recollect!'

Like molten excrement in the guts, malodorous and obscene memories, a whole generation of them, roiled the President's insides. He recollected his orphanhood after his father's passing, the desolate paths of the pimp, the painted faces of his sisters, the slights at the hands of strangers, the sad and stale suppers, and then the rabble, the demagogy and the incendiarism, and at last the Palace! But who guided him along this tortuous path, clothed him and fed him and sustained him, and turned his infamy into uprising and power? Who liquidated his sisters' keepers, assassinating some and slandering the rest, so that the history of the dynasty could be re-written without hindrance? Shakuni, Shakuni had done it all! *But,* thought the President *I will overcome these memories, I will break free!'*

'I do not want to remember,' whimpered the President. 'I will have you liquidated.'

'If you do that, the Confederate and Tartar secret services together will depose you.'

The President sank into despair; the mess of memory, persistent slime, now filled his insides to choking; his lips twitched and his eyes welled with tears.

'I see you grieve,' Shakuni said. 'Believe me, my Lord, I have seen the excrement of history and know the sorrow of sovereign power.'

The President became calm and said, 'Help me, O Shakuni.'

'I will, my Lord. Be at peace.'

'But Shakuni, Paraashara has not been taken yet.'

'Why must you fear, my Lord? His insurrection will soon be contained.'

'It is not him I fear, it is his King.'

At this the wily Envoy grew thoughtful, and said after a long silence, 'Know this, my Lord. Age after age, power prevails over justice. Some decrepit historian in the future might vindicate Siddhaartha and judge you harshly, but we will not be there to read his tome, and what is more, another injustice will be triumphing then.'

'It may well be,' the President said, 'but fears assail me.'

'I shall dispel your fears. If you so desire, I can request Samarkhand to escalate the Sorrow.'

'It is no use, Shakuni, the people's enthusiasm is waning.'

'There is a way, my Lord. If Samarkhand would co-operate, we can move into nuclear Sorrow.'

The President's face lit up. 'The nation will be grateful to you, O Shakuni. Samarkhand and we will detonate low yield nuclear devices on each other's outlying provinces and all will be well.'

'Hasten slowly, sire. There is a catch. Even the smallest nuclear device will spread radiation, and then neither the Confederacy nor Tartarland will buy our meat. You must remember that we are not the only Third World nation in this trade. We have competitors.'

'No one told me about the competition. My Council of Ministers kept me in the dark.'

Gone were the thoughts of nuclear splendour from the President's mind, and confused and dithering once again, he said, 'What now, Shakuni?'

'There is a way,' Shakuni said. 'Let me undertake another secret journey to Samarkhand.'

*

The following week the news of nuclear war broke in Dharmapuri and Samarkhand. Dharmapuri blamed Samarkhand, and Samarkhand Dharmapuri. Tremors of patriotism shook both the peoples.

The resident Confederate spy in Shantigrama reported to his headquarters, 'We can continue to export the meat as usual from Dharmapuri as well as Samarkhand. There is no danger of nuclear contamination, as the most lethal ingredient in this war is saltpetre. Do we expose this?' He was advised not to destroy the facades of friendly nations. The Tartar spy received similar advice.

'It is a primitive joke,' the *Wild West Times* commented, 'a parody of war.'

This put no dent in the truth as they saw it in Dharmapuri or in Samarkhand, the decolonized truth of the black and brown continents.

*

Yet the truth sprouted in the white cities themselves, in the cities of the greedy alchemy; it sprouted in the quickening of the dormant seed of the forest. In a Confederate city, the wife of a captain of industry spoke to her husband. 'I do not want this, God knows I do not!' Her voice shrill, pained, she went on,'I cannot bear it. I cannot.'

Her husband faced her unhappily, for had he not done it all for her love? He had hired master alchemists to invent venoms for the Peninsular war, agents that would cauterize the forest shelters of the yellow foemen; he-had driven his workhouses to unremitting labour, and seen his profits grow.

'I did this in desire for you, my beloved,' he said. 'What is it that you cannot bear? Now at last, our men of alchemy have found a way of recycling life, and what is more, for the first time in history, we share this discovery with the Tartars.'

She began to cry. He took her in his arms; she was still in his arms when a black maid came in with a tray of steaming food. Cannibal flavours, compelling, rose with the steam, scents of ancient killings and spits and woodfires. The flavours assailed her and destroyed her resistance. She cast a furtive glance at the tray, catching a glimpse of the delicate dressing, the mimicking of fruit and flower, and shrank back in dread.

'Ah, my husband,' she said, 'these are black and brown children!'

Her husband picked up a forkful of food from the tray, and resumed his relentless kissing of her on the neck, on the breasts, on the lips, prising her lips open with his, and slipping the food into her mouth. The mouth slavered in primitive arousal, its juices spilled over the lips; she heard far away a mother lamenting her child's death. The seduction on the tongue grew frenetic; she closed her eyes, and in despair and pleasure, like virgin sinning, swallowed her first mouthful. Another mouthful, and yet another; now she was crying and eating off the tray the flesh of humans from the black and brown continents, processed by the alchemists and transfigured into peaceable fruit and flower. She cried out deliriously, 'Hold me, my husband!'

They made frenzied love, and as sleep came over her, she said,'The thought of our children fills me with anxiety. Go, my husband, and find them.'

Saying this she fell fast asleep. Her husband rose from her, and paused to contemplate her beautiful body: breasts with the sensual sag of middle age, arms slender and thighs fair, with down curled between them like a mountain orchid. This was the body of the white woman, of the white mother and lover, the body destined to triumph in the last war of the races.

He wound his way up to the floors above, and then to the attic, in search of his children. As he knocked on the attic door, suddenly a heavy foreboding came over him. The door opened and he looked on the wild tableau in dismay: his son and daughter and their lovers, naked, garlanded with flowers, rose to greet him.

'God, my God!' he said.

'If you come in peace, father,' his son said, 'be our guest.'

On lotus leaves, spread on the uncarpeted floor, were fish and loaves. The son pointed to these and said, 'Father, an ancient offering. Partake of it.'

'Alas!' his father said. 'In vain have I bestowed on you the fruits of my alchemy; in vain the wheels of my workhouses turn night and day for you.'

'Night and day, indeed!' his son said. 'They turn out toxins!'

'Alas!' his father said. 'My seeds sprout wild. The forest strikes root in my very home.'

'Not in your home alone, father,' his daughter said. 'It strikes root in your workhouses and your highway and your cosmodrome. It is the uprising of our King.'

'Your King!' exclaimed their father.

An unseen presence listened, it laughed gently; the laughter rose, transcendent, and lapped against them like the tides of a lake on a mountain side.

'Our King,' said the daughter, 'Siddhaartha.'

'The brown King of the wretched!' A great rage seized him. 'Ah, cursed is my progeny!'

The son spoke to his father accusingly, 'This is the War of the Wounded Plants. Recall to your mind, father, what your toxins did to the forests of the yellow people: leaf and bud and sprout were cauterized to death. Witness the miracle of their second coming, the forests avenge themselves, sprouting in this attic, in our minds.'

'No more!' said his father. 'No more!'

His son lunged at his sister, and seized her by the wrist.

'Come, my sister!'he said.

Together they fell to the boards of the floor, over the spurned offering of fish and loaves; she simmered in that forbidden embrace, her breasts the buds and sprouts of the forest, and her tresses the fire of the toxins. Darkness came over the father's eyes like the blight of his progeny; then the fires seared through it and his eyes became festering wounds; the wounds cried out. He turned and fled, stumbled on the stairs and fell, rose and groped again. The vision of sin, the grim fire-sacrifice, moved on before him.

CHAPTER XXV

The Crystal Prisons

Men who fear the sunrise and the wind, reflected Paraashara in forgiveness, *these are your twin discoveries: trade and war. In these have you barred the light and touch of God.* Armies faced each other in battle, as in a mart of trade, with death as their tender; ants and worms, burden-carriers of the mart, heaved their tiny loads of flesh from the trenches, and hurried back and forth across the simmering line of battle.

Paraashara walked the captive Hayavadana along the mountainside, where, in dugouts of snow, the soldiers kept vigil; the dead, their fingers frozen around their weapons, kept vigil over their own decomposition.

'Look Hayavadana,' Paraashara said, 'so many cadavers! and so much hide promises good trading.'

'It does, indeed, General, sir.'

'Imagine the fine things we can make with the hide, and the travellers who will come here to buy them.'

Hayavadana now felt at ease with his captor. He volunteered, 'We could do many more things to please the travellers, sir. We could set up state-run bordellos. Women in cages would undoubtedly excite the travellers. It would help them experience their own brutal past again.'

'Great will our earnings be, in precious hard currency. What then might we do with all that money?'

Hayavadana smiled at the thought.

'Sir, we can import candy and toys.'

'What else?'

'Guns and rockets, flying machines and machines to ignite nuclear conflagrations.'

'What else?'

Hayavadana forgot his captivity as the guns aroused his lust.

'Concubines, sir,' said the man-woman.

'Concubines?'

'Yes, sir. We make Sorrows so that we can buy the guns. The gun-sellers would reward us for buying from them, they will give us much gold. With that gold we can pay for more concubines.'

'The story of the wealth of nations?'

'So it is, sir.'

Then Paraashara hit Hayavadana. Hayavadana fell.

'Get up, you dog! You, this country's Minister of War!'

'Yes, my Lord.'

'Ill-begotten one!'

'My Lord...'

They walked on. The unshut eyes of the dead soldiers were turned to crystal, and in them were frozen phantom images of grief and loss: the smiles of children and the bodies of woman wrenched away from the act of love. The mountain sun fell into the glacial crevices of the crystal and turned into cold rheum.

'Hayavadana,' Paraashara said, 'can you look within those eyes?'

'My Lord...'

'Can you? Speak!'

'Mercy!'

'Well then,' Paraashara said. 'March!'

God, prayed Paraashara, *free me of my kindness.*

Paraashara asked, 'From where does your army launch its attack?'

'Further on, my Lord,' Hayavadana said.

They walked on; the mountain's veins of snow glistened like silver.

'Over there, my Lord,' Hayavadana said, 'our Persuaders march towards the border, seeking the enemy.'

From the eyes of the dead soldiers, the women and children imprisoned within the crystals, cried out to Paraashara and, with their cries ringing inside him, he said, 'Hayavadana, order your soldiers to cease fire.'

'Ah, my Lord!'

'Order them!'

'My Lord,' Hayavadana said in consternation, 'that would be treason.'

A frenzy seized Paraashara; he kicked Hayavadana in his vitals; Hayavadana fell, his seeds spilt and blood oozed from his mouth.

'Get up, dog!' said Paraashara.

In agony the Minister of Sorrowing rose and stood before Paraashara.

'Tell them!' commanded Paraashara.

And, his frenzy unpacified, Paraashara cried out; the cry, wild primordial, echoed down the mountains, and the icons in the dead eyes listened. *Orphaned ones,* he cried, *I throw open your crystal prisons, I crush the seeds of the men who orphaned you!*

The frenzy exhausted him, he limped along behind Hayavadana towards the front-line, and called out, 'Persuaders, see your Minister of Sorrowing!'

The soldiers saw their Minister bleeding from his genitals: with bugles and trumpets they did him obeisance.

'Speak to the soldiers, Hayavadana,' Paraashara said.

Hayavadana spoke slowly and painfully, 'I, your Minister for Sorrowing, command you to cease fire.'

The Persuaders listened baffled; they broke ranks and stirred in disquiet, but then a great levity of realization came over them.

'We are free!' they cried. 'We are free! Our Minister sets us free!'

There was no more army, no more country, only freedom; their guns slung across their shoulders, they turned and began a playful trek down the mountain. Paraashara saw this and was pleased, the elemental anger quietened within him. After the last of the columns had disappeared, Paraashara turned towards Hayavadana.

'Alas, Hayavadana,' he said, 'I see you pant.'

Hayavadana fell to the ground again and Paraashara stooped over him.

'My Lord,' Hayavadana said, 'like any other Minister, I too was humble once. A scullion boy and male whore. And like any other Minister I too wore the mask of a leader.'

'Ah, Hayavadana, I see you die.'

'My Lord, forgive this humble one.'

Hayavadana's eyes closed and his mouth fell open. The whore's lips repelled Paraashara, yet tenderly and in forgiveness he moistened them with snow.

Then Paraashara descended the mountain path towards his encampments.

CHAPTER XXVI

The Wayside Scrub

The mountain slept, and in the grottos that were Paraashara's bivouac slept Mandakini and her comrades in arms, Aryadatta, Ghrini and Sreelata. Paraashara himself stayed awake. Beneath his wakefulness the cheerless knowledge of victory turning into sour defeat grew like a kernel of soul-sleep. The soldiers whom he had freed were coming back to battle. For the President! They had left their women and children behind; war called them back to the trenches like a regressive and obscene vice. They found shelter in the trenches, and the ant and the worm waited once again in the marts of death.

My sin has been punished, thought Paraashara, contrite, *the sin of my own war. I took up arms, and so I disobeyed my King. O Bodhisattva, your laughter does not well within this mountain when we most need it. Have I choked its subtle spring with my sin?*

Paraashara was looking out expectantly across the looming shadow of the mountain, when a mighty flash lit the night and the thunder of weapons shook the skies.

'My General,' Mandakini said, waking, 'what shatters so rudely the sleep of the mountains?'

'My sin,' Paraashara answered in sorrow.

*

People fleeing their new found freedom, in terror of the sky and the silent night, of breeze and birdsong, sought once again the insane celebration of excrement. As the citizens went back to their debasement, the soldiers to their trenches and the workers to their polluting workhouses, spectres of ancient darknwith them.

A rocket streaked across the sky like an incandescent serpent. It fell amid the peaks, and the valley lit up with a forest fire like a sunrise in the night.

'Ah, Mandakini,' Paraashara said, 'the war resumes.'

He rose and strolled, listless, down the mountain path. After a while he looked back and found Mandakini and her comrades coming after him.

'General,' Ghrini said, 'tell us what we should do.'

The skies thundered again and the horizon was dotted with lesions of fire.

'General, our's is a blighted species with no future. I am not blaming you or the King. Look at this suicide that is written into our genetic substance. People demanding war, women craving widowhood, and children, destitution. Tell us what we should do.'

'Go back to the bivouac, Ghrini.'

'And where are you going?'

'A long way. A long, long way.'

The drone of flying machines rose and fell. 'General,' Mandakini said, 'what shall we do back in the bivouac?'

Paraashara came forward and held her in his arms: Mandakini enveloped his lips with a kiss. She said, 'We shall go with you. Our bodies are beautiful; in them may you overcome your sorrow.'

Paraashara forbade her to say more.

'General,' Sreelata asked, 'are our times ending?'

Paraashara pointed again to the bivouac, and said, 'Go!'

The General watched them go and his eyes grew dim with tears; he watched them disappear into the bivouac. Then he turned and walked down the winding track.

*

A hundred leagues to the north of Shantigrama, on extensive

'General,' Ghrinlands levelled by machines, stood the newest of Dharmapuri's workhouses. It had been pasture land before, with fruit groves and peasant hutments. The Partisans of the Holy Spirit had pitched their tents there and harangued the peasants on the miracles of the machine and the bounty of alchemy; they had dazed them with song and chant, and persuaded them to give up their holdings to make way for the workhouse. The peasants grieved to part with the fields they had tilled and the orchards they had tended, but their grief mingled with the chant, with the din of the absurd. They prised themselves out of the dense wet earth of their numberless generations, and scattered into inhospitable wastes. And the land they left behind became inhospitable itself. The machine and the chemical were upon it, the trees were gone, and the living clods changed to hardened and laid-out surfaces. Over this, proudly, rose the funnels of the workhouse. The villagers came back now and again, in their desultory foraging, to the hard, flat workhouse yard, where their dead still dreamed and mouldered. They came to the workhouse's barred gates and looked on in awe and wonderment. Among them one day was a villagers from deeper inland.

'My brethren,' Vedavrata, the villager said, 'Siddhaartha's insurrection will undo these workhouses.'

The straggling trash exclaimed, 'Truly, then, this King is a reactionary!'

'But think, my brethren of the village,' Vedavrata said, 'have not the workhouses despoiled our pastures and the groves where our children once plucked fruit?'

'They have,' the villagers grew angry as they spoke. 'But they did so to earn us much-needed exchange.'

'They sullied the skies...'

'Of what consequence is that?'

'Brethren, I come from Gurugrama, the village of the ancient teacher, which is wild country. Before my village was despoiled by tradesman and alchemist, its women had large breasts and they made love long and deep. But our trees are gone, and so are the shades; our foods are shipped over the seas for money. Thus, denied the canopy of trees and the fruit of the earth, the breasts of our women have shrivelled and their loving become feebler.'

'You speak incoherently, aborigine. You have turned insane.'
.'I want my fruit trees.'
'Do you not desire the country to be wealthy?'
'I do not know, I do not know.'
The listeners broke into derisive laughter.

'Laugh, my Brethren,' Vedavrata said. 'Yet I shall tell you what I do know with my body: I need blue skies above me, and winds that are pure and free. I desire the destruction of whatever thwarts this.'

When the stragglers laughed again, their leader spoke, 'This is no laughing matter. Let us remember that the Red Tartar Republic will be the largest producer of coal by the turn of the century. Do you realize that, aborigine?'

'I do not,' Vedavrata said.

'On whose side are you, aborigine?' the leader demanded. 'On the side of the toiling majority or...'

'I do not know, sir. All I know is that I want the free breezes and fruit trees and women with large breasts. I am certain, gentle masters, that you want much the same things.' Before the leader could say, *No, it is hard currency we need,* the rabble said, 'We too, aborigine.'

'Well then,' Vedavrata said, 'on which side are *you?*'

At this the rabble grew dispirited, and one among them spoke, ignoring the leader, 'We do not know.'

'But I know, gentle masters. Siddhaartha will come, and if he is repudiated, will come again, and undo this workhouse and all the workhouses.'

'Not this one. No one can do that. This workhouse is the President's own.'

'Whoever owns it,' Vedavrata said, 'what goes on inside it is the canning of human meat.'

'Treason!' the leader cried.

Like one who conducts an orchestra, he waved to the rabble, which broke into rhythmic chanting: slogans for the workhouse and for the bounty of alchemy.

*

The State of Dharmapuri stepped up its efforts to tap the reservoirs of patriotism. In garish exhibitions were laid out Persuaders' corpses, embalmed and resplendent with medals. On gilded platforms sat the live exhibits: heroic orphans, naked and jewelled widows. The people looked on and lusted for war. Frozen in a cage of glass was the split skull of a Persuader; women were overcome with martial fantasies of their men lying on the snow, their skulls split into pink hemispheres; they lusted for widowhood. Men imagined their genitals shorn from them by flying sharpnel, they lusted about their wives whoring in the cages. In the mystique of the State, men and women chanted, they clapped and sang and danced round the exhibits, living and dead.

*

At the gate of the exhibition a little boy stood crying. He told the guardsman, 'Sir, I hear they exhibit children inside.'

'Go away, go away,' the guardsman said impatiently.

The boy did not stop crying, and the guardsman, relenting, answered him, 'Yes, they exhibit children. But they exhibit only orphans.'

'I too am an orphan.'

'Did your father die in the Sorrowing?'

'No, sir. Both my father and mother are alive.'

'How can you call yourself an orphan then?'

'My parents have disowned me. They had sent me for canning, but the managers of the workhouse turned me down.'

'Why, my child?'

'I was diseased.'

The guardsman was now full of sympathy. 'Alas, my child, that was truly a misfortune. But under no circumstance can we export diseased meat and sully the fair name of the country. And since you are not truly an orphan, we cannot put you on exhibition either. It makes me sad to think that you are of no use to anyone. Go back to your father and mother, and live off the pickings of their kitchen.'

At this the child broke into a loud wail. 'I cannot, sir. They will deny me even those pickings, because I have failed my country.' He dried his tears and went on, 'I shall take medicines and make myself whole and go to the workhouse. I do not want to fail my country.'

*

The people bore the knowledge of war and canning within their patriotism, the dismal tract between memory and oblivion; along it they were led, driven, in the manner of beasts of slaughter. The dust rose behind the herd as it moved at a slow, hopeful trot, stretching its myriad necks to nibble at the scrub on the wayside: the lustreless growth of the printed word, the headlines, the slogans and pledges, the plans and statistics, the advertisements for toys and appliances. The herd had visions of its destiny in these, it smiled to itself and thus contented, its heads bent down, trotted on.

CHAPTER XXVII

The Revelation

Dusk was on the river; the Jaahnavi flowed golden, nibbling the earth of her banks. The fires of war seeped through the forest; when the last seed and shoot were burnt down, the river would renew it all in its perennial becoming.

Siddhaartha sat beside the flowing water and meditated. In his meditation he came to a wondrous place of infinite distances. He saw a many storeyed edifice rising tier upon tier, its distant cupola lost in the clouds. The King entered through an archway; the corridors were long and dark and through their tunnelled reaches he heard the speech of tribes and clans, voices that rose and cascaded into a deep quiet. He climbed up a flight of stairs and reached the first storey where sat bemedalled men.

'Commanders and Generals,' Siddhaartha called out, 'who desires war, and who profits from it?'

They sat still without lifting their heads and answered in deep melancholy, 'No one has asked this till today.'

'That very reason impels me,' Siddhaartha said.

'What folly!' the Generals said; the sick old men wheezed behind their medals. When they tired of Siddhaartha's persistence, they said, 'Go up to the next storey and ask.'

Siddhaartha climbed up to the next storey where he found alchemists at work. They too said, stooping over their potions,'Go up to the next tier.'

The King climbed again, and came to where great merchants sat and contemplated wealth. 'On to the next floor,' they said.

Again the climb, again the melancholy evasion: *Up there. Climb yet another tier!*

In those many tiers of the edifice sat all the masters of the world. Before each of them Siddhaartha laid bare his torment: *For whom were the wars fought, and who, in the end, profited from the holocaust?* Behind the epic happenings of every war were people, and a man behind the people, a woman, a home, a child, the mathematical reduction of a final answer. This answer eluded him, and he climbed on.

The lone questioner seared the collective courage of those who sat on each tier; they too became lone men, and the terror was upon them of the billowing smoke and the bleeding wound. Yet they would not answer, and so pointed their fingers up. *How many tiers have I climbed?* thought Siddhaartha, *Oh, how many?* From his vertiginous foothold Siddhaartha looked down; over the earth, distant and small, set a strange ancestral sun. Pursued and fugitive, the earth orbited through this sunset.

Siddhaartha climbed again; this was the last of the storeys. This was where all the masters had pointed.

Siddhaartha called out, 'I have come!'

The last of the masters, residing unseen beneath the cupola, replied, 'Oooooh.!'

'I have come,' Siddhaartha said again, 'I, Siddhaartha, the Bodhisattva.'

'Aaaaah!' came the reply.

'Who are you, O King of Darkness?'

'Aaaaah!'

'Speak to me, for every artifact of my civilization pollutes the air I breathe, the armouries bristle, the creatures of the earth move toward Armageddon, unaware. O Master who hides, you have the answer. Tell me: who desires war, who profits from it?'

'Oooooh!'

No, it cannot be a mere echo, Siddhaartha thought as he reflected on the sinister and mysterious voice, *this last tier cannot be untenanted.* Siddhaartha was sure of the presence of the Master of them all, there on the uttermost height of the citadel, above the orbit of the earth, amid the spangled tinsel of the skies. For hadn't it been to this awesome throne that the thousand masters of the world had pointed?

Siddhaartha climbed the last flight of steps which led to the throne in the cupola. There was no one on the throne! From the foot of the desolate throne he peered into the darkness of the cupola. Then suddenly torn parchments rained down on him; Siddhaartha's poise faltered, and the mighty edifice swung.

'Ah!' Siddhaartha cried. 'Is there anyone here? Answer!'

'Aaaaah!'

'Who is responsible? You?'

The mystic echo again, 'Oooooh!'

Then Siddhaartha saw: he gazed in disbelief at the dimunitive and decrepit thing that clung to the arches of the cupola, and with gnarled digits shredded the ageing chronicles of the earth. Its fangs flashed white in simian chatter and its eyes looked down in imbecile evil. This then was the keeper of the riddle of war, this misshapen gene that sat over the clans and races of men. Darkness thickened in the bowl of the cupola and hid the beast. Now came the answer that he had hoped would unlock the secret that moved the armies and the sovereigns, in an echo that swirled out of the cupola like a hollow and· insane wind,'Oooooh!'

Siddhaartha turned away from that demonic void and began his toilsome journey of return, a great sadness upon him, a pure and tender despair; and pursuing him down the interminable spiral that bored its way back to earth was the echo of the cupola.

*

Jaahnavi, Siddhaartha told the river, *I have woken from a dream. Beloved Prince,* the river said, *we wake from one dream into another.*

Her currents bore away the dream images; Siddhaartha opened his eyes to the cold breeze.

Every enquiry, said the river, *takes you to the Genesis. So too the answer you have sought.*

The King looked up at the skies, towards the crystal precipices of space whence the Jaahnavi sprang to journey to the earth. His quest ended, he grew calm. Beside him the river flowed, timeless.

CHAPTER XXVIII

The Last Warrior

Laavannya lay on the slabs of the prison floor; she had been raped over and over by her captors; the slabs grew cold, and the wound between her thighs simmered red; pain surged like a sea-tide against those red shores where rafts of sperm lay strewn. In blindness and despair, smothered generations cried out from the wreckage. And, as they lay dying, Laavannya ministered to them the scents of motherhood.

*

Siddhaartha and Paraashara were together again by the riverside; the distraught General spoke, 'O King, they put my armies to rout.'

'Did we not foresee it, Paraashara?' asked Siddhaartha.

'You did! Why then did you lead us all this way?'

Siddhaartha spoke in gentle admonition. 'Paraashara, you succumb to feebleness.'

Bitterness came over Paraashara, and regret. 'I ought to have known it, my King. Defeat awaits the one that follows the Seer.'

'One may comprehend defeat in many ways. Now you are doing it your way, the way of the General.'

Paraashara's eyes turned to the city far away. Smoke was rising from its workhouses once again, and the excrement of the great machines came riding over the river, triumphant. In grief he turned away from the sky and the waters, and faced Siddhaartha. 'See, my King: the canning of little children! See the slag of their bones float down the river.'

'I see it, Paraashara.'

A flight of airships sailed overhead, filling the sky's caverns with their deep rumble. Paraashara spoke as the sound died away,'Children become orphans; women in their prime, widows; men have their vitals torn out. How could they crave such consummation?'

'Know them, Paraashara. This is *Leela,* the play of the Great Delusion, and they are but wafted along on its tides.'

'Ah, do these words come from you?'

'Indeed, they do, Paraashara.'

'Unwise Bodhisattva! They took Laavannya prisoner, and raped and killed her. They carried away Mandakini and Sreelata to the soldiers' whorehouses, and young Ghrini to where men come lusting after other men.' A great turbulence churned Paraashara. He fell to the earth with a loud cry, and covered his face with his gnarled, soldier's palms.

Looking up again at Siddhaartha, he said, 'The very people we freed, deny us. They go back and offer themselves up for insane slaughter. You will call it *Leela!* It is incredible, my King.'

Siddhaartha smiled. 'It is no more incredible than the Chosen One who takes on the sins of men. He too desires his immolation in exactly the same way.'

The playful smile left Siddhaartha's face. 'It is far from my mind to mock you, Paraashara. But know this from me: the frivolous maker of history and the dim-witted subject who follows him into senseless war and death are both seers, chosen ones.'

Paraashara asked bewildered, 'Seers, my King?'

'Indeed so. They rise and perish not in history, but in the great paths of destiny; they put themselves through endless becoming to cleanse the Godhead.'

'What strange atonement! For the sins of God!'

'For the fond Play of the Manifest God.'

A tremor seized Paraashara. 'Ah, my King, take hold of me, for my mind flounders.'

In the resonant voice of the Bodhisattva, Siddhaartha called, 'Come, my son!'

Paraashara obeyed. Siddhaartha drew him to his bosom. Paraashara lost himself in the King's embrace; standing thus he looked into the distance: at the workhouse funnels, totems risen into the horizon to offer a lurid sacrifice; beyond the funnels the crimson spread of sunset; and beyond it the starways and the footprints of disconsolate Avatars.

The embrace ended.

The Bodhisattva's face shone in the sunset. Paraashara stood gazing long-on that face, then sank to the earth and pressed his forehead to the dust of the Master's feet. Now the knowledge came to Paraashara, tender and sad. 'So, this is the Hour, my Teacher?

The Hour of Parting?'

The Bodhisattva's love flowed over the soldier in great tides.

'It is Paraashara. But I shall be there by the riverside when you seek me. *Swasthi!**

Paraashara sat where he had knelt, his limbs grown still. Siddhaartha walked the path up the river towards the sunset. As Paraashara gazed after the departing Master, the cold light of the sun filled his eyes and then a darkness came over them; when he could see again, the path lay deserted.

*

Somewhere inside a workhouse, on a conveyer belt enormous as a highway, Sunanda lay washed and naked. Before him and after lay countless children. Some sobbed, yet others struggled to get free but were kept down by powerful force-fields. Muffled commands sounded in the chambers below, and the belt began moving. Sunanda did not struggle and was not afraid; he sank into a deep quiet, a sleep full of lucid knowing.

A vision came vivid to him in his sleep, he saw his passing and his recurrence. His body had changed and was food. Around the

*A traveller's benediction, a boon of peace and grace.

food a family sat: a man and a woman and a girl of tender age, her eyes blue and innocent and her cheeks fair as the mountain snow. Sunanda communed with the girl: *Fair one, my elements come to life again inside you. Whether you are asleep or awake, or lie dreaming in the day, I shall recount to you the ancient sorrow of my race. We flowed out of the matted locks of Shiva, you and I, together; then we coursed down our different ways, in streams that were clear or muddy with the silts of the earth. Now, in this partaking, the streams come together again.* Tears welled in her blue eyes and fell down her cheeks. *Brother,* she said, *I receive you into me.* Said Sunanda, *Fair one, this is our new and everlasting covenant.*

The conveyer belt moved faster. Sunanda woke from his stupor once, just once did he cry out for his father and mother; as the cold blades of the saws raced towards him, he said, *Merciful sister, here I come.*

Paraashara awoke to his loneliness and orphanhood. He did not know how long the swoon had lasted: the rain had fallen and dried on him like the tears of the Bodhisattva; the sun had set and risen and had risen again and was setting.

Then he saw it before him, resplendent and miraculous: a great *pipal* tree risen from the moss and the bare stretches of the river bank. Paraashara lifted his gaze to its majestic canopy, and tears streamed down his face. He kneeled down before the tree, he flung his arms around its trunk. 'Siddhaartha, my King,' he cried, 'is this you?'

Each twig and leaf trembled in response; in tide upon tide its deluge gathered over the uncomprehending Paraashara.

'Speak to me, my King!' Paraashara implored.

The tremor of the twigs and leaves ceased, and the Great Pipal fell silent beside the eternal Jaahnavi. Alone beneath the great Plant, the warrior sat and sorrowed for the sins of the Beast, he wept disconsolately and long. And the weapon, slung over his shoulder, lay quiet, like a child that had cried itself to sleep.

Glossary

Avatar: A human incarnation of the Divine Principle

Bodhisattva: An evolved being on his way to Buddhahood

Gobernadors: Governors

Shaakuntala: A classical Sanskrit play by Kalidasa based on the mythological story of Shakuntala, daughter born to a faerie woman and a sage. Shakuntala was abandoned in the forests and was raised by birds

Shakuntaas: The forest birds which raised Shakuntala

Siddhaartha: Not the Buddha of history, but a parallel creation

The Jaahnavi: The sacred river Ganga (Ganges) personified. She is believed to spring from the heavens and flow down to the earth

The Pipal: A large and spreading tree of great longevity; it was under such a tree that Gautama meditated and attained Buddhahood

The Red Tartar Republic: The former empire of Tsariana, a sprawling territory, which the Great Midsummer Revolution turned into a Republic. Guided by infallible dialectical-and-materialist sorcery, the Republic claims to be the natural ally of all decolonized peoples. The Communard Party, which led the revolution, holds paternal sway over Communards the world over. Gives Dharmapuri solidarity and slogans

The White Confederacy: A trans-oceanic capitalist-imperialist power practising the sorcery of consumerism and hardsell. One of the traditional'enemies' of Dharmapuri, the Confederacy yet replenishes Dharmapuri's armouries, and supplies the President with candy.